"Eng...

to dramatic effect. . . . [She] has brought to light one of history's more daring and fascinating characters, cracking her open to show what it feels like to live within the swirl of such influence and in such a pivotal and interesting time."

—*The Washington Times*

"Ephron's sense of place is strong and vivid throughout *White Rose*."

—*The New York Times Book Review*

"An intense love story and a satisfying adventure tale . . . *White Rose*, set in Havana, Washington, D.C., and New York, drips with atmosphere. Period details abound. . . . The reader will emerge the richer from having been immersed in a story that resonates with immediacy despite taking place a century ago."

—Gannett News Service

"A vivid embellishment of a true account, Ephron's story is quick and lively."

—*Kirkus Reviews*

White Rose
una rosa blanca

AMY EPHRON

White Rose
una rosa blanca

A NOVEL

BALLANTINE BOOKS

NEW YORK

A Ballantine Book
Published by The Ballantine Publishing Group
Copyright © 1999 by Amy Ephron
Reader's Guide copyright © 2000 Amy Ephron
and The Ballantine Publishing Group,
a division of Random House, Inc.

The poem "Una Rosa Blanca" from *José Martí: Major Poems*, bilingual edition,
translated by Elinor Randall and edited by Philip S. Foner (New York:
Holmes & Meier, 1982). Copyright © 1982 by Holmes & Meier Publishers,
Inc. Reproduced with permission of the publisher.

White Rose is a work of fiction based on a true event. The author would like
to acknowledge the help of the Cuban Studies Desk at the Otto Richter
Library at Miami University, and Karl Decker's and Evangelina Cisneros' own
accounts of their story. In some instances, the author has chosen to use Miss
Cisneros' own words.

This edition reprinted by arrangement
with William Morrow, an imprint of HarperCollins Publishers, Inc.

Library of Congress Catalog Card Number: 00-191292

ISBN 0-345-44110-9

Manufactured in the United States of America

First Ballantine Books Edition: October 2000

10 9 8 7 6 5 4 3 2 1

For

Maia, Anna,

Ethan, and Lila

Cultivo una rosa blanca
En julio como en enero,
Para el amigo sincero
Que me da su mano franca.

Y para el cruel que me arranca
El corazón con que vivo,
Cardo ni oruga cultivo:
Cultivo la rosa blanca.

—JOSÉ MARTÍ

I cultivate white roses
In January as in July
For the honest friend who freely
Offers me his hand.

And for the brute who tears from me
The heart with which I live,
I nurture neither grubs nor thistles,
But cultivate white roses.

—JOSÉ MARTÍ

Casa de Recojidas
The Prison for Abandoned Women

Havana, Cuba
September, 1897

$\int$he was seated at a table in the center of the prison yard, in a straight-backed chair, the legs of which were slightly uneven and wobbled uncertainly against the coarse and rocky soil. The table was roughly carved so that if she was not careful where she placed her hands, she would come away with splinters.

She sat perfectly erect, barely moving, holding her head high, chin slightly down, breathing, in small measured breaths because the acrid smell of female urine, intensified by the sun which beat down relentlessly in the open patio of the *Recojidas,* was not one you could ever get accustomed to.

She longed for the slight shelter of a palm tree, to walk barefoot in the sand, to let her feet be cooled by the crystal blue water as the soft waves crashed lightly into shore. She wanted to breathe the moist tropical air, lightly scented with flowers, the air of her childhood, that she knew still existed a few blocks away.

She was dressed in a high-necked, concealing, long-sleeved dress that did little, however, to hide her lithe form, incongruously, as if it were a few years ago, and she was on her way to tea at the big house on the plantation. They had brought her the dress that morning, freshly ironed, so that she would appear to the public to be better treated than she was. The dress still smelled faintly of the carnation water she used to sprinkle on so liberally. She wondered what they had done with the rest of her things—if one of the guards' wives wore her black lace shawl at night and someone else was reading her Bible and playing with the beads of her rosary.

She had dressed carefully and pinned her hair up, squeezing her cheeks to try to put some color in them. It suited her to go along with them, to present an image of respectability.

It pleased her that they were a little afraid of her and afforded her certain liberties that they did not allow the other prisoners—that they would still let her have some discourse with the outside world.

There was a composure about her, a peacefulness, way beyond her years and certainly curious in her present circumstances. She was still young enough not to be frightened of anything, despite what she had been through.

She was staring straight ahead, her eyes intently fastened on the entrance gate. She wanted to see him when he first came in, this journalist who was coming to see her, who had been sent by Mr. Hearst to interview her.

She was aware of everything around her—she had been trained to this, long before she was imprisoned. The cluster of black women in the corner passing a lone cigarette between them, their torn dresses draped about them with little attempt to conceal their bodies, as they stood hunched defiantly against the thick walls that towered high in the air, well within the sights of the lone guard, posted atop the parapet, armed with a Spanish rifle. They had seemed to her, at first, so fierce, these black women, as though they, too, were an enemy faction, something else to be feared. But that was before they had earned each other's respect. Anna, the oldest of the prisoners, standing off to the side alone, nervously shifting her weight from one foot to the other, as if she were a child, her gray hair hanging scraggly about her face, her pale blue eyes almost as translucent as her skin. For murdering her husband, she had been sentenced to life, a life that would no doubt be cut short by her sentence. It was said that in the moment when she took his life, she lost her will to communicate with the outside world. It was Anna that Evangelina understood the most, how violence was the only way that she could think to silence him, how when she neatly slit her husband's throat with a hunting knife, as if in penance, committed herself to a world of silence. The other women, seemingly educated gentle women, who stood apart by their background, there for the same reason that Evangelina was—because they or their father or their cousin or their husband or their neighbor believed in their country, their right to a free country, more than in anything else. It was that belief, that naive conviction, that gave her what little composure she had.

Would she tell her story again? Yes. She would tell it as many times as she had to. *Viva Cuba Libre.*

*H*e was surprised at how pretty she was. He hadn't expected her to be so pretty. He had seen the photograph that ran in *The Journal* and others, when he'd gone through her file, but they were grainy and her hair, done in the fashion of the times, even though pinned up, fell a bit about her face obscuring a clear view.

He hadn't expected her to be so delicate or refined. He had thought the last three years, first when she was incarcerated with her father on the Isle of Pines and then imprisoned on her own in Havana, would have shown more marks on her, visible marks.

He was surprised, also, at her—complacency was the wrong word but there was a dignity about her, unexpected in one so young. She was only nineteen. And yet her spirit, visible in her eyes, in the way that she took everything in in a moment and her agility, evident even though she was seated, indicated something stronger and wild, if pushed. He wondered if he would be able to trust her. Trust was always fairly tricky with someone who believed in a cause more than in anything else. And if he would be able to get her to trust him.

Better not to reveal too much, at first. Better to maintain the facade that he was a journalist and had no purpose other than to interview her. Better to let her tell her story in her own words, that would be the best way for him to get a sense of her.

She was soft-spoken, no hesitancy in her voice, as if she'd considered all of this before and knew how she would answer him.

"To begin with," she said, "I am not a girl, as all the people who have been writing about me always say I am. I am a woman. I am nineteen years old."

He resisted the impulse to smile or even tease her, better to acknowledge the cultural differences between them. And there was a sensuality to her, a confidence that was not the least bit girl-like.

"I was born in Puerto Príncipe, the capital city of Camagüey. It's in the mountains, inland. And you, in

America, call it the Kentucky of Cuba. I think they mean by that that we have beautiful horses there . . ."

By this last, he recognized that she had a sense of humour then and an understanding that we, in America, try to explain everything in terms of ourselves.

"Puerto Príncipe is a little city, very self-contained, self-sufficient, and we were very happy there, there were many happy people there before the revolution." This last was said with no remorse, just a statement of fact that this was what they had come to.

"I am the youngest of three daughters. My father had a little money, and we lived in a pretty house with thick walls to keep out the sun and a courtyard with a fountain in it. It was in this courtyard that all of us children learned to walk. That's the first thing I remember, holding myself up against the edge of the fountain, made of white clay with tiles that shined turquoise in the daytime and seemed a darker blue by the light of the moon. The water leapt and sparkled in the sun and I used to think it was alive and try to catch it and make it stand still and talk to me. It seemed to me as if the water was dancing. I dream about the fountain now and the courtyard which is so different from this one."

She looked over at a group of women standing watching them, the other political prisoners, her compadres. "I can't let them know that I'm afraid," she said. "They all look up to me." She studied his face to see if this would draw him to her, play on his sympathy somehow, this image of her as a young girl with too much on her shoulders . . . but he was poker-faced. He was good. It would take more than this to get to him. She wondered if he only responded to women who were inaccessible. How could she be more inaccessible, more unobtainable, than behind bars? By holding back from him.

"After my mother died . . . ," she said, "I never knew my mother, I was two, although my sisters have told me about her. After my mother died, my father was never happy in Camagüey. He couldn't bear to stay in the little house where he took her as a bride. So, he sold it . . . and we went with him from one place to another, as if we were gypsies, all over Cuba. We were a bit like gypsies, the three of us girls. My father"—she laughed when she said this—"would have been better pleased if *one* of his children had been a son. And, I think, since I was the youngest, his last chance for one, it fell to me.

"He often looked at me, took my head between his hands and said, 'Evangelina, when I look at your brow, it seems to me you should have been my son and not my daughter.' I would laugh and start to whistle." And, in that moment, she put two fingers up to her mouth and gave a whistle as if she were a sailor on a street corner that shrieked through the prison yard and cut the slow air with its sound. That surprised him.

The largest of the black women standing against the wall turned and gave her a nod and all the other inmates seemed to stiffen and stay in one position as if they were waiting for something and Charles Duval (whose real name was Karl Decker although she did not know that at the time), the man from New York who had come to interview her, truly felt as though he were in alien territory.

Evangelina Cisneros put her hands at her sides again and sat there, demurely, and continued as if nothing strange had happened. "My father," she said smiling, "would cover my mouth, instantly, with his hand, it was almost like a game with us, for in Cuba it is not good for a girl to behave like a boy."

"He treated you more like a son than like a daughter . . ."

"In many ways, yes. My father always spoke to me freely and without reserve and through him I knew something more of the world than most Cuban girls, who are brought up in the seclusion of their homes, ever dream of knowing."

He wondered what else she had been taught.

"We moved finally to the town of Cienfuegos on the Southern Coast of Cuba to a sugar plantation where my father had the job of foreman. And for us girls it was idyllic, almost like living in a doll's house . . . until the end, when it was time to throw away the doll's house."

He should be taking notes. He was going to have to file a story, whatever else he did. Her imagery was quite good. ". . . throw away the doll's house." He realized she *had* considered how to tell this . . . The guard on the parapet was watching them. Evangelina's eyes flashed darkly and she began to speak more quickly.

"That last night," she said, "I think of it as the last night because it is the last night we were truly free, although we had committed to something that made us no longer civilians, that last night we had to act as though it was a party. We had to make it look as though we cared about nothing except eating and dancing. My sisters and I cooked for two days, sopas, beans, fresh bread, bunches of plantains that we were planning to bake fresh lime juice we had squeezed to mix with the little bit of rum that Papa had. That's the last thing I remember, looking at the bunches of plantains that hung in the kitchen as though it was a normal Friday night. The three of us girls weren't enough, so, we invited Lourdes and Maria and Mrs. Diaz and the two Lopez daughters. There were thirteen men. All of them Cuban except one who was a Mexican." She said this last harshly as though she would like to spit the word instead of say it.

He had heard it was the Mexican who had betrayed them. "Tell me about him."

"I never knew his name. But I get ahead of myself. A few nights earlier, my father had come home as he usually did just as the sun was setting. Carmen and I had made supper. But he did not kiss me when he walked in the door. He did not speak to either of us. We knew—we had heard my father and his friends sitting in the shadow of the house whispering—that there was to be a war in Cuba. When my father didn't speak to me, I knew that something had happened. 'Papa, what is it?' I asked him. 'What's wrong?'

"He ignored me at first and sat down to eat his supper. All at once, he pushed away his plate and jumped up from the table. He caught me by the shoulders and looked directly in my eyes. 'Wrong. I don't know if anything is wrong. It would be wrong not to . . . I am going to fight for Cuba,' he said.

"There was no hesitation when I answered, 'If you are going, Papa, then I am going with you.' Will you write that in your newspaper, Mr. Duval? Do you dare? Will you tell them that I am not a young girl wronged. That I was a part of this." She stood up. The interview had ended. She did not wait for a guard to accompany her. She walked away from him into the walls of the *Casa de Recojidas*, the Prison for Abandoned Women in Cuba.

Evangelina, don't turn away from me. How can I get you to understand that we are on the same side?

Damn her. Did she think this was a game? And then there were two Spanish guards upon him, two more came from inside the prison and lifted up the table and carried it inside. The interview was definitely over.

They escorted him out. The gate closed behind him. The heavy bolts rolled shut and then something like the sound an organ makes after it has sounded a note which reverberates through a chapel and holds the air, as the locks were rolled into place and the metal scraped against metal. A closing note. He turned and looked back at the

12

Casa de Recojidas, the Prison for Abandoned Women. She was inside there somewhere in a cell. Did she have a window, was she looking out at him now? The stench of the prison was still around him, overwhelming him as the sun set over Havana and the ground, for a moment, became warmer than the air.

Damn her. Didn't she know how hard it had been to get in to see her in the first place.

The day he arrived in Cuba, she had been placed *incommunicado*. There was no coincidence there. Most likely, she didn't know that. Visitors were not to her a regular occurrence. He had gone about his business. Gone to the office every day, filed a few stories pro forma, made discreet inquiries, applied to see her, spread a little bit of money around . . . Did she think they wanted her to tell her story? Perhaps they did. Perhaps they were using him, too.

He would file a story in the morning, something that would please them and anger her.

He was ten blocks away before the sounds and smells of the city replaced those of the prison, smells of salt water fish, fresh bread, gardenias, and good cigars. He sat at one of the tables at *Las Olivas*, the outdoor cafe in the Plaza, ordered a Cuban cocktail, cognac and soda, and waited for Eduardo.

$\mathcal{E}$duardo Cortez lit a Cuban cigar. "Make no mistake, I do this for money. I risk my life only for money." His eyes darted around the room as he spoke but in a manner that seemed a part of his frenetic nature rather than the surveillance that it was.

"You see that girl over there?" He turned and looked in the direction Cortez had nodded, a beautiful young Cuban girl. Her name was Ana Maria Varona and her hair was wild about her face, her shirt cut too low in the front so that the curve of her breasts was visible. She was sitting with a girlfriend laughing, her shoulders swaying as if she were about to break into a dance. For a moment their eyes met and he saw something else in her stare.

"She doesn't work for money. We will pay her but that is not why she is here. Which one of us do you trust more?"

He had to think about this.

"I'll answer for you," said Eduardo. "I will tell you the right answer. Me, because I am not willing to die. Which one of us should Evangelina Cisneros trust? She should trust no one.

"Her sisters are in a small fishing village with a woman who is pretending that she is their mother. Costanza has a baby. A little girl. Alicia. They say she looks very much the way Evangelina did. They're safe. For now. Tell her this news and she will start to trust you. You must ask her where her father is. You must get her to tell you where her father is. Should she trust you? She should trust no one. But if you do your job properly, she will never know that. You see, she's valuable either way. Possibly more dangerous if she dies. If José Martí had not died, then none of this would have happened . . . She will think that I am her friend. But, believe me, she should trust no one."

*E*vangelina fell asleep and dreamt she was in Cienfuegos. The soft wind blowing across her face ripe from the sea. The air fragrant with the smell of salt and coconuts. There was a baby crying in the yard . . . and someone was singing it a lullaby. Her sisters were laughing. She could hear them but she couldn't see them. *Carmen. Costanza.* The day turned into night and everything was pitched in darkness. *Papa. Papa.* And then she was running. And someone was after her. She could hear their footsteps. And then she was on the beach, riding a horse, bareback, holding on to its chestnut mane. The full moon above casting a soft glow and enough light to see by. Carlos was beside her on Silver. He turned and smiled at her. And then the beach was pitched in darkness. And she was thrown.

When she woke up, she was aware of a rhythmic pounding as though someone was banging a sharp object against the bars.

"Anna. Anna. Is that you?"

She tapped against the wall. The banging stopped and a moment later, she heard a humming noise, frantic, almost like a bee. "I know, Anna. I know. You didn't mean to. Sometimes there isn't any other choice. You just did what you had to do. Sometimes there isn't any other way out."

The humming noise got deeper and almost melodic. "I know, Anna. I know."

Washington, D.C.

*W*hen Katherine Decker came home, the house was empty, that eerie quality a house has when it's been left, quickly and without preparation. She saw the closet door was slightly ajar, his suitcases were gone and on the bedside table, he had left a note. She sat down on the bed to read it. The house was still, quiet. She heard the sound of her own breathing. Outside the window, the American elm, tall, majestic, casting a shadow on the sidewalk as the sun set, almost as if it were a protective blanket. It had rained the night before and the air was crisp, clean.

As always, he had left her a note.

Dear Katherina,

I've had to leave (unexpectedly been called to New York, Julian Hawthorne has summoned me), and from there, I'm not sure where. I will send you a letter back and let you know when I expect to return. (Weeks, I imagine, this time.)

I will think, all the time, that you are by my side. I will try to dodge whatever bullets come my way. And know, when you sleep, that I am next to you.

Your husband,
Karl

She held the note (as though it would somehow tell her more, where he had gone, where he would be sent to, this time) tightly in her fingers and read it again, as though the simple act of reading it would somehow keep him close to her.

She had known when she married him that he was a journalist. That he had spent time in South America, in Cuba, had lived in the mountains for three months with Gomez and some of the other revolutionaries while working for *The Journal*. Other women's husbands worked. Some of them quite hard, but not like this. Ralph Thomas, Emma's husband, sometimes stayed on the Senate floor till all hours (although they had their suspicions that there was something else involved, rumours about that he was a bit of a ladies' man). But his schedule was predictable, he was never that far off.

Emma could always track him down if she really wanted to. But living with Karl was something else. She never knew when she would come home and he would be . . . gone. Or *how long* he would, in fact, be gone for. Or where he *had* gone.

Her sister Tess insisted that was part of the attraction. And, in the beginning, that might have been true.

Karl was terribly handsome, not in the way of other boys she had been raised with, there was something rougher about him, strong-shouldered, competent, dangerous, with those pale eyes that seemed to see through everything he witnessed and seemed to her to hold depths of understanding for everything that came before. He was well-travelled, but not in the usual society way— he could tell you about the mountains of Peru; the coast of Spain; he had travelled deep into parts of Africa; he knew things about politics and the way present-day politics related to earlier times, almost as if he were a historian, and yet he conversed with a certain passion she had never come in contact with before.

Yes, that was part of the attraction, at first. But as his disappearances had become more frequent, the accompanying anxiety about his return had also grown measurably.

"Not tonight, Katherine," she chastened herself softly. "Don't do this to yourself tonight." Nathan would be ready for bed and waiting for her to tuck him in. Marguerite would have given him his bath by now. And brushed his hair, still wet, slicked back across his head.

That little angel face staring up at her from under his covers waiting to be kissed. Better not to let him know how much you missed his father. Don't do this tonight. Marguerite has left a lamb in the kitchen and small roasted potatoes and peas sprinkled with butter and fresh mint. And there's that little slip of an Edith Wharton book on the bedside table. Take it down with you. Pour a glass of port. And when you go to bed, say a prayer that he will return to you safely, as he always has before.

That was three and a half weeks ago, and she still had had no other word from him.

Havana, Cuba

The next time he saw Evangelina, she seemed thinner. Her face pinched, small lines of worry in her forehead, dark circles under her eyes.

"You look as though you haven't been sleeping."

She laughed at him. "I dream that I will sleep by the sea," she said. "And then my dreams are interrupted."

"I have news for you," he said. "Wait. I cannot tell you now. They are watching us. You speak."

"What do you want me to tell you about?"

"All of it." He opened his pen so it would look like he was taking notes. He would take notes. He would continue to file stories.

"Where do you want me to start?"

"After they arrested your father . . ."

She took a breath. "After they arrested my father," she said, "we didn't know what we were to do.

"He was riding back from the cane fields. It was early morning, the morning we were to leave . . ." She hesitated. It was harder to tell this than she had thought it was going to be. She had told it once before, to Mr. Bryson, but then there had been an urgency to the telling and she had let him write it as he wanted. The result of that had been—a death sentence to Ceuta.

Decker sensed that she was having difficulty. "Is this hard for you?"

She didn't answer him at first, so he went on. "We could talk of other things," he said. "I took a walk this morning on the beach. The water was pale blue, almost turquoise, and so clear, you could see through it to the ocean floor. Is it like that everywhere in Cuba?"

"No. In Batabanó, where we spent the night on the wharf, before we were transported to the Isle of Pines, the ocean turns from black to white. It is said that it frightened Columbus' sailors—they thought it was a portent of evil—but really, it is just the churl fish caught in the waves, making the water appear black, and, when they free themselves, the wake of their foam turns the ocean white—even the fish frightened the Spanish.

"It would be harder for me not to tell this. But you must—promise me that you will listen.

"It was the morning that we were to leave to join the others in the mountains . . . and my father had gone to the fields to make it appear as though there was nothing unusual . . .

"The Spanish soldiers found him there. They hit him in the back with the butt of their rifles, tied his hands behind him, put a rope on him as if he were cattle and made him walk along behind them, laughing when he fell down in the dirt. I understand he begged them to let him come to us and tell us he was leaving but they had no humanity.

"They found on him—papers that gave the whole plan of our uprising, for this he will not forgive himself, which led them to the others. We have tried to tell him that this isn't true. No es verdad, Papa. No es verdad. They already *knew* about the others from the same man who told them about him. But he holds himself responsible. From him, I have learned that you never write anything down. From him, I have learned that you must be very careful what you say.

"Do you always write the truth, Mr. Duval? How do we know that what you print is the truth?"

He needed her to trust him.

"Come closer." The guards had walked away from them but only for a minute. He must speak quickly. He was aware of the way she smelled as she leaned her head in and his lips all but touched her hair when he spoke. "Costanza has a baby. A little girl. Alicia."

She said it after him, "Alicia."

"They say that she looks very much the way that you did when you were little. She's in a fishing village with your sisters and a woman who is pretending to be their mother. Will you—will you tell me where your father is?"

"I have not seen my father since the Isle of Pines."

"That is not what I asked you."

She sat up straight and looked at him directly. "You will be very careful what you write about me, Mr. Duval." It was almost a question. And then she smiled at him. He realized it was the first time he had seen her smile.

And then the guards were on her again and their interview ended abruptly. He watched as her face became porcelain, her figure docile, as she allowed them to lead her away. She knew better than to turn back and look at him. He waited until she disappeared inside the *Casa de Recojidas* before taking his leave and wondered how much he would be able to tell her.

$\mathcal{A}$ double-life. He'd been doing it for so long, it should have been second nature to him. Easier in Washington where secrecy (or was it sub-text) was a way of life and whispered conversations held in private smoke-filled rooms were often more binding than those on the Senate floor, or, at least, laid the groundwork for what was to be publicly accounted for. In D.C., it was easy to hide or at least become part of the backdrop of educated men, politicians and lobbyists and journalists in suits, who were simply doing their job. An American in Cuba, while not an oddity, was more discernible.

Just there on the corner. She was looking at him with very big eyes. "Por favor, Señor. Por caridad. Tengo hambre." She looked hungry. Her dress was torn. She had bare feet. She couldn't have been more than six.

Just there on the corner. Outside the Hotel Inglaterra, the American helping the beggar girl. Making quite a show of it, as he reached into his pocket for some pesos and centavos. He wanted to take her down to the market and buy her a dress but that would be too much show, too noticeable, too recognizable. Better just to appear an American in passing who probably had a child at home who missed him.

Nathan would just be getting home from school, his socks dirty from the play-yard, crumpets and weak tea with milk waiting for him on the kitchen table. A ham sandwich if he wanted it or one with cucumbers.

He reached into his pocket to give the girl another handful of change. It was like a magician's sleight of hand, to appear to be doing one thing when, in actuality, you were doing something else.

He lingered at the desk in the lobby at the Hotel Inglaterra, patiently—while the woman in front of him negotiated a bicycle for a trip to the seashore the next morning—then loudly asked for his messages and room key, loud enough so that the man sitting in the chair behind him smoking a Cuban cigar, his face hidden by that morning's paper, could hear him. Decker stopped in at the bar for a brandy and soda, Spanish brandy. And then surveyed the room in the mirror conveniently placed behind the bar and took careful note of the two Spanish Generals entertaining the three Cuban girls at a table in the corner. Or were the three Cuban girls entertaining them?

He took the stairs up to his room on the third floor, taking the first flight, slowly, so that everyone in the lobby, including the fixture, the heavy-set man behind the newspaper, could see him. He'd seen the heavy-set man before, sitting in the back of a carriage outside the *Casa de Recojidas,* and suspected he was an officer in the Guardia Civil. He wondered if the Cubans were watching him, too, and if there were ever a moment when they would help him (and risk a certain death, why would they do that?).

He left the door open to his room, briefly, so that anyone passing in the hall could see he was about to retire. He took his shoes off and, in his stockinged feet, went out into the hall, and left his shoes outside the door for the Negro to shine them while he "slept". He went inside and put his boots on and lay down on the bed. He should write a letter to Katherine but he would do that from the office in the morning.

Julian Hawthorne had given him a small parcel of books on his departure, a slim volume of Rubén Darío, some articles by Stephen Crane. He read for awhile then turned the light out. His thoughts went to Katherine.

That she deserved a better husband than he was presently able to be. It wasn't fair to her. She thought he was a journalist. She didn't know there was another side.

It went along with their slogan:

While others talk, "The Journal" acts.

It was only a month ago that he'd received the note. (Only a month to him, how long would that seem to Katherine . . .)

Hawthorne wanted to see him. He couldn't imagine why this time. The note had read simply:

Your presence requested in New York. Discretion advised. An assignment that will take some time.

Respectfully,
J. Hawthorne

He arrived in New York at 4:02 and went directly from the train station to *The Journal*'s offices downtown. "Mr. Hawthorne has been waiting for you," the young clerk told him as soon as he arrived.

Julian Hawthorne was one of those men who had always appeared old. Karl imagined he wasn't more than ten years his senior but he had always seemed old, had always been quite serious about everything and had about him what Katherine would call "an aura of responsibility." He had an efficient no-nonsense manner in keeping with the deadlines that he met each day. There were no niceties, barely even an acknowledgement of his presence.

A slight nod of his head and then, "He wants you to go to Havana."

He was WRH. William Randolph Hearst himself. Why now?

"He wants you to go to Cuba. Immediately. We've booked your passage on a steamer that leaves from Miami in three days' time. You will be travelling as Charles Duval."

"Spell it please."

"D-u-v-a-l. A journalist from our Boston office, sent to be the replacement for George Eugene Bryson."

Decker had heard that Bryson had been ousted from Cuba for stirring up a mess about that little Cuban girl.

He looked at Mr. Hawthorne inquiringly and waited for him to go on.

"But that is not why you are there . . . You are being sent to rescue—don't look at me as if I've lost my mind—to effect the rescue of Evangelina Cisneros."

He thought drily to himself, *While others talk . . . "The Journal" acts.*

Rescue, had they gone mad?

He knew the next few words by heart.

"Money is no object. Hopefully, you will be able to buy her way out. The guards are bribable, don't you think? We do not wish to put you at risk. But if you have to break her out, if that's the only choice, I know that you won't fail. If you would prefer that we send someone else . . . but there is no one else appropriate."

He was referring to the time Decker had spent last year in the mountains with Gomez and his men. He knew his way around Cuba, knew a number of people in the resistance who would protect him, was fluent in Spanish, and had masqueraded as someone else before.

"We have no other recourse. At least that's what we feel. They have sentenced her to twenty years' imprisonment at Ceuta." (Ceuta was the Spanish penal colony in Africa where no one ever survived.)

"Why would they send a woman to Ceuta?"

"Why would they send anyone to Ceuta . . . ? You must not tell Katherine why you're leaving or where you've gone. She knows if she needs anything, that she can contact me."

Had she contacted him by now?

He lay on the bed with his eyes open. Could he trust that it was quiet. He could hear someone laughing down the hall, a man, deep, guttural belly-laugh, punctuated by a woman speaking quickly, and then a door slam. He waited another moment. He was very aware of the sound of his own breathing. He took out the slip of paper the little beggar girl had handed him in exchange for the centavos. On it was an address which he committed instantly to memory. He held the slip of paper over the candle burning on his bedside table and, when the note had been reduced to ashes, got up and put his hat on.

He opened the door to the hall and stepped out. Halfway down the hall, he lit a cigarette, so that if anyone were to see him on the outside staircase, he could pretend he was simply getting some air. He slipped outside through the window onto the stone balcony that edged the hotel and crouched down silently until he was certain nobody had seen him. He took the rope from his pocket, fastened it to the iron grill, nautical knots, and let himself down to the balcony on the first floor. Then he stood on the ledge, untied the rope, hoisted himself over the railing and jumped down to the street, still staying as close to the building as possible so that his form would be obscured by shadows.

Tonight would be an exercise to see how easily he could slip through the streets of Havana and return to his room undetected.

The beach was deserted. The town was empty, the streets still, the houses vacant, like a ghost-town.

Is there anybody there . . .

Where were the women that had raised her?

Cecilia, the wife of the farmacia, who sold fresh fruit juice, tepid, the temperature of the fields, and Cuban sandwiches, thick slices of ham on day-old bread, at a stand she'd set up in the back of the store. Cecilia, who always smelled of cinnamon and cornmeal, her apron stained with flour and grease, who swore she could tell a person's mood by the color of their irises, if they were angry or happy or sad. Cecilia, who thought sunshine and pineapple a cure for everything . . . if she could only bottle it. She laughingly called it Mama's elixir and said she would sell it in a blue jar, azure blue. Cecilia, a catch-all for local gossip because of her station, always knowing who was ill, who was born, who was in trouble.

It was Cecilia who had come to warn them early that last morning. Too late. She had seen the Spanish soldiers on horseback, riding through the cane fields, the morning sun not yet high in the sky on a day that would be too long to get through. It was Cecilia who had crouched and hidden in the cane watching as they rode quickly and steadily up to Evangelina's father.

She watched the Spanish soldiers prod him in the back with the handles of their swords, and then their rifle butts, until he fell helpless to the ground, tying his arms behind his back and then his feet, then pulling him upright and prodding him again with their rifle butts to get him to move, laughing as they watched him fall in the dirt on his face.

It was Cecilia who had come to the house to tell her they had taken her father. Her eyes big and brown, the irises yellow, the color of sadness.

Where was she now? Why was there no one in the town? *Carmen. Costanza. Cecilia. Maria.* Have they taken all of you?

She woke up and remembered. "Costanza has a baby.

A little girl." They say she looks very much the way that I did when I was little.

Her father was in the mountains. With Carlos. If she ever got out of here, she would go to the mountains . . .

$\mathcal{I}$f anyone had been paying attention, they would have noticed an empty house on O'Farrill Street, just opposite the prison, had been rented the week before. *La Lucha*, the Havana newspaper, recorded the rental, innocently noting that "The lessees could find no one to become responsible for them, so they paid two months in advance." But in truth it was gold pieces, freely offered with no other discussion, that secured the lease. And, it was its location, directly opposite the *Casa de Recojidas*, which made it a desirable property.

Preparations were made for it to be "occupied." One of Eduardo Cortez's boys, a colored Havana native (his skin appearing all the darker as his pants and arms were

36

spattered with white paint), arrived carrying a bucket, brushes, and a ladder slung over his shoulder. He left the door to the little house open almost the whole day. He made quite a show of whitewashing the walls of the house, ate his lunch on the outside stoop, and, a few hours after dark, tired, dusty, spattered with a great deal more paint than when he'd begun, he left, leaving his ladder behind, the purpose of the exercise all along. A little table had been moved in, four chairs, a cot, and basic cooking utensils, but as yet, no one had taken up residence.

Decker would not go to the house tonight. He would walk by to see if he could get there undetected. The air was thick and not much cooler than it had been in daytime. He heard footsteps behind him. And then stiletto steps. He turned and saw a young couple, doing a spontaneous dance, and then the man caught the woman in his arms and kissed her. There was the sound of an argument coming from inside the bar on the corner, broken glass. He kept on walking.

The *Casa de Recojidas* is in the lowest quarter of Havana, edged by rows of squalid huts in which live Negroes and Chinamen. Two cultures so disparate, their children never play together in the street. Their languages have nothing to do with each other, the strange patois of the Negroes with its African accents and peculiar combination of French and Spanish, and the foreign staccato monochromatic tones of the Chinese. If they had their way, the adults, too, would have nothing to do with one another although they are forced to by trade and proximity, the Chinese seeming always to have something to sell, surreptitiously in doorways or in the corners of the razor-thin alley that zigzags, almost moat-like, around the prison. Decker had walked the alley daily so that each corner of it was familiar to him, the smell of it reeking whether the sun was out or not. And by nightfall, when the rats were visible in the gutters, roaming freely, eating from the trash that gathered there, it seemed to him that he was somewhere beyond the end of the earth. And that Evangelina was just on the other side of it.

If anyone had stopped him and asked what he was doing there, he had, in his pocket, an address of a Chinaman who was to sell him some herbs for a stomach ailment that was in danger of keeping him up most of the evening. But no one noticed him except the rats and they didn't seem to mind that he was there.

*I*t surprised him that they allowed him to come each day. Evangelina looked tired. He knew better than to ask her if she wasn't sleeping, how could she be. She seemed stoic, almost as if she had given up hope.

"I had no choice about any of this . . . I feel in some way as if it was all decided for me. That once a certain course had been set, the rest of it was inevitable. Unless I changed who I was. But what good are principles, Mr. Duval, unless one is willing to live and die by them?

"After they took my father," she said, "it was days

before we knew what they had done with him. And then we weren't certain. It was rumoured he had been put in a jail in Cienfuegos.

"I made a little dish of huevos and put it in a basket with some fresh oranges and a cake that Cecilia had made and walked to Cienfuegos to see my father. But they would not let me in. It was almost as if the guard was playing a game with me. We didn't know if my father, although we tried not to think this, was alive. I begged the guard to tell me if my father was there. But all he would say was there was an older man there who no longer knew his name, perhaps he was related to me and perhaps he was related to someone else.

"My heart stood still at this. Had they beat him so badly, he no longer knew who he was?

"I gave the basket to the guard and said, whoever the man was, perhaps he was hungry. I asked the guard if he would, please, see that the man got it and say that Evangelina had been there to see him and that I would come again. He said that he would do this and I was surprised (although I shouldn't have been surprised) when I turned back to see that the guard had taken the napkin off the basket and was helping himself to what was beneath.

"After that, each morning, I would make two portions, one for the guard and one for my father. It is not a bribe, if it is given freely. Don't you think?"

He answered her, "I think sometimes it doesn't matter what we do to get what we want."

"Oh, but in that you are wrong, Mr. Duval. There are some things that should never be used as trade."

He looked at her face and thought what he would give to be as young and principled as she was . . . He knew, of course, what she was referring to.

"Do you know where your father is?" he asked her.

"Sometimes, my father can be difficult to find."

"We have discovered that."

She almost smiled at that. "Should I continue?"

"Yes, please."

"After a week or so, they let me into the jail to see the man. I was frightened that first time I walked into the prison, almost as if I had a premonition, that they would not let me out.

"That first day, the guard kept watch—they would not let me be alone with him. The relief I felt that it *was* my father was tempered by the realization that he no longer knew who he was. I tried to be gay. I told him news of home. Only trivial things. That the chestnut mare had had a foal. That Pedro, who he'd always liked, was paying a lot of attention to Costanza. My father seemed not to see me, as if he was in his own world. He looked much older than he ever had before. I tried to put his mind at ease about us. I told him that Mr. Beauchamp, the man who owned the plantation (pronounced the American way, 'Beecham'), had said that we could stay there as long as we liked, at least until there was a trial. It's an American principle, is it not, Mr. Duval? Innocent until proven guilty. But even the mention of Mr. Beauchamp's name did nothing. He just looked vacant.

"Actually, it was Mrs. Beauchamp who had interceded for us. Mr. Beauchamp had called us over to the big house and once there had said, 'Harriet, what do you think we should do with them?'

" 'Well, I don't think we can be putting them out on the street. I couldn't have it on my conscience that I'd sent three innocent girls into the world unchaperoned.' I didn't tell her what our part in this had been. She'd known us since we were little and, I think, still thought of us as children. I didn't tell my father this detail. The guard was listening to my every word and I didn't want to bring any harm to the Beauchamps.

"I told my father that we missed him, that he could be proud of us, that we were earning our keep. He didn't seem to hear anything I said. That we got up each morning and checked the fields. That everyone was working almost double-time to protect us, keep the plantation running, and to make it seem to the Spanish as though nothing out of the ordinary had occurred, and that our spirits were intact. And when I told him that, he put his fingers up to his lips, the way that I had when I was a little girl, and pretended to whistle."

She did it again to show him what she meant.

"And it was as if that was our signal—he was letting

me know that he could hear me, that he really *was* all right—that he'd understood everything I'd said and that he was just pretending for the guards that he didn't understand a thing. I think, so he did not have to answer any more of their questions.

"He smiled when he did it and barely a whistle came out, just air, but I knew that he was all right. He showed no emotion when I took my leave.

"When I walked home, the afternoon sun was directly overhead, my legs felt weak and I knew, when I was halfway there, that I was ill. I had barely slept since they had taken my father—we used to lie awake worried they would come for us, counting the hours between dusk and dawn. I had forgotten to eat that day myself. Or else it was, finally, since I knew he was okay, I could show how worried I had been. I collapsed on the side of the road.

"I don't know how long I lay there before Cecilia found me. She said I wasn't making any sense. I kept thinking the basket was a hat and trying to put it on. She lifted me onto her horse and rode with me in front of her back to our house. She made me a drink of li-monada, lemons and water with fresh sugar cane to sweeten it, and then went to get her husband. He could recommend nothing for me but salt tablets and rest. I think what frightened them was that they could wake me but they could not get me to stay awake. I think I slept for four days. Carmen and Costanza took care of me, spoon-feeding me as if I were a baby.

"It was two weeks before I could get back to the prison to see my father. He made no pretence. This time, there was no charade. His face was like stone. He took my hands in his through the bars the moment he saw me. 'Evangelina,' he said, 'you are a soldier's daughter and now you must carry yourself like one.'

" 'I have never done otherwise, Papa.'

" 'I am sentenced to be shot.'

"I tried not to show in my face what I felt. I think my heart stopped beating. *Shot? When? Would it be a public execution?* I could not live with myself if I did not do what I could to stop it.

"I went to the Spanish headquarters. I wasn't in my right mind. I asked to see the Captain-General. The guards laughed at me. They told me the Captain-General would not see me. That he was busy, tired, not there. They all said different things at the same time. I collapsed on the steps and cried. They laughed at me all the more and told me when the sun melted the earth, perhaps I might have an interview then with the Captain-General.

"But I went back the next day. This time I put on a dress. I wanted to look—" She searched for a word. "I wanted to look innocent. I took a long time putting my hair up. I wore the little cross that Mama had left me on the gold chain around my neck. The soldiers laughed at me again and one of them called me 'puta araberella,' 'whore of the streets,' but, as he did, a young man was coming up the steps and sharply reprimanded him. The man turned to me and asked me why I was waiting there. He took my hand. He told me he was the son of the Captain-General. I told him that I wanted to see his father, that my father had been sentenced to death and that I had come to ask for mercy, that I had come the day before, and that I would come each day until the sun melted the earth, if that was what it took, and the Captain-General would see me.

"He told me to come inside with him. I waited in a big tiled hall while he went into the inner offices. But his father would not see me. The young man told me he himself would do his best to get his father to be lenient. And that I should come back again the following morning.

"My sisters and I sat up all night, as if we were keeping a vigil. We burned candles. We tried to remember what it was like when we were not expecting a war. I could not have slept if I'd wanted to.

"I went back to the Spanish headquarters in the morning and found the young man waiting on the steps for me. He handed me a paper. And, as he did, he took my hand and kissed it. I never even knew his name. I was surprised that he had tears in his eyes . . . until I looked at the paper.

"He had been successful, in a way. My father's death sentence had been commuted. He had instead been sentenced to life imprisonment at Ceuta, the Spanish penal colony in Africa, where I am to be sent now. You know its reputation, don't you—that no one ever survives."

Don't worry, Evangelina. I won't let them send you to Ceuta. But he could not say this to her out loud.

After a moment, she went on, "My father's health was such that I did not even think he would survive the journey to Ceuta." Her voice cracked as she said it.

"Is this hard for you, Evangelina?"

"It would be harder for me not to tell it. I—thanked him. I tried to fall to my knees to thank him but he caught my elbow and held me up. I wanted to thank him because he had bought me time. My father taught me that if you take things one step at a time, take each as a small victory and keep on going, then all things are possible.

"This next part will surprise you. My father had been transferred to a prison in Havana to wait for the next transport ship to Ceuta when we got word that there was a new Captain-General. General Weyler. Your newspaper calls him 'the butcher.' Here, in Cuba, we call him 'El Matador.' But he was very kind to me, at first. I'm not sure why. Perhaps he felt my father was more valuable to him alive than dead." Her voice got hard when she said this. "Perhaps he felt he still had things to learn from my father. I mean this not in a philosophical way," she laughed at herself, "but in a way of espionage.

"General Weyler had just arrived in Cuba and we

were all naïve enough to think there could be a peaceful solution. He had taken up offices in Havana at the Palace. I went to Havana to see him. When I presented myself at the Palace, they let me in immediately. As I said, General Weyler had just arrived and was trying, still, to have us in Cuba think that he was courteous and kindly. To me, he was, that day. He offered me coffee as if I were a visitor, which I declined. He listened to what I had to tell him—that my father was an old man, that he was weak and frail, and that he would not live to be transported to Ceuta. He didn't ask me any questions. He seemed already to know who my father was. When I finished, he nodded his head once, and turned to his secretary and said: 'Give her an order to have her father transferred to the Isle of Pines. Your father will be safe there,' he said, 'until the war is over.' He turned his attention then to papers that he had on his desk, ignoring me, until the order was written and he signed it. He handed it back to his secretary who handed it to me. I tried to thank him but he held his hand up, signaling that he wanted no further speech from me, and he turned his chair around so that his back was to me. I think I danced all the way to the prison where they kept my father. Can you imagine dancing all the way to any prison?"

He almost smiled at that.

The sun was falling low in the sky. The *Casa de Recojidas* was covered in mist. It seemed to him the guards must have forgotten them (or else they were busy

47

with someone else). They had never let them talk this long. He let her go on for a little while and then interrupted her. "I think we should put an end to this today, Evangelina, so that they don't feel we have abused the privilege."

She nodded at him, acknowledging the sense of this. "I do feel it is a privilege to speak to you," she said and then she smiled. He left her sitting at the table alone waiting for the guards to escort her back to prison.

*E*duardo Cortez was standing in a doorway on the corner on the opposite side of the street, his face partly obscured by shadows and a wide-brimmed hat, which he pulled down even farther when he saw Karl Decker walking toward him. Once he was confident that Decker had seen him, he pulled the brim of his hat farther down on his forehead, as if it were a signal, and began walking briskly on his side of the street a few hundred yards ahead. Decker followed, making certain that it did not appear that he was doing so.

A block and then another and then a left turn. And then, in the middle of the next block, Cortez disappeared into the door of a luggage shop. Decker walked to the end of the street, to try to ascertain if he were being followed, but there was no one on the street except an old woman sitting on the stoop of an apartment building. He crossed at the corner and doubled back, stopped and stared in the window of the luggage shop as if he was examining the wares before walking casually into the store. The shop was empty. He was aware of the sound of bells when the shop door closed behind him.

After a moment, a woman appeared through the curtain that led to the back of the store. Her hair was pulled back, severely, and she had large silver earrings in her ears and despite her age, she must have been close to sixty, it was evident she had been quite beautiful when she was young. Decker managed to get a glimpse of her ankles, which were still quite shapely and in heels.

"What can I do for you, Señor?"

"I am looking for a gift for a lady," he said, "something not too intimate."

She threw him by taking a billfold out of the display case.

"A gift for a lady . . ." That had been their agreed-upon catch-phrase. Why wasn't she taking him into the back of the shop where he was certain Cortez was waiting for him?

"This should be what you are looking for," said the Señorita settling on the stool behind the counter. "It's very soft. The quality is excellent. And it can hold many things."

"I am not sure it is what I am looking for."

"I have nothing more to show you. 30 pesos, Señor. Why take more of your time when you have found just the thing? Do you want me to wrap it for you?"

"Whatever you think," realizing in that moment, he had best defer to her judgment.

She wrapped it, prettily in tissue, and put it in a box, and tied it with a velvet ribbon. "Would you like a card?"

"No, thanks," he said, "I'll use my own."

He was aware of the shop bells jingling slightly as he shut the door behind him. The streets were crowded. People were just getting off from work. The cafes were filling up, women were lining up at the outdoor fruit stands and spilling into the street from the open door of the panadería, shopping for supper on their way home, easy to get lost in the crowds, difficult to tell if he was being followed. He did not notice the heavy-set man, his shadow, disguised as a taxi driver, sitting in front of a carriage-for-hire, idly watching him.

$\mathcal{Y}$ou look as though you've seen—something in a dream," said Nadine, the large black woman whose bed was next to Evangelina's in the cell. They slept four in a row, her, Nadine, a tiny Cuban woman named Ceci, who was in for theft, and Maria, whose face was as plain as the hills except marked by sadness as her husband and children had been shot the morning she was arrested. "And I hope," Nadine went on, "you're not thinking about that New York boy. You got no business thinking about him."

Evangelina smiled. She had noticed, for the first time that day, his shoulders, and how kind his eyes were, how strong he seemed to be, how competent. She wondered where he lived and allowed herself a particularly female thought—if he had a wife somewhere and children who were missing him.

Her father had always said that you could tell if a person was lying by their mouth (not by their eyes, as some people thought, but by their mouth), it would stiffen a little before they spoke if they were lying. She knew he was lying to her about something but she didn't know what. She thought she had his sympathy. She thought, also, that she had his respect. She could not see why he would want to hurt her. Americans, despite their prurient curiosity, seemed to be their friends, even if their motives were not entirely clear.

There were many in the revolution who believed the Americans had their own agenda (they had tried to purchase Cuba from the Spanish three times before), but without the help of the Americans, it was possible that they would never end this war, not that the Spanish were ever going to win it. It was a struggle that had been going on since Columbus had set a cross into the beach at Cape Maisí in 1494. And, despite the presence of 250,000 Spanish troops under the command of Weyler (the entire population of Cuba was only 1.1 million), the insurgents in the hills were holding their own.

She was starting to feel a little bit like a spider under glass, about to be put on display. If only she knew what they really had in mind for her. She wondered if he would help her, if she asked him to.

"You're pining . . ."

"I am not." Evangelina denied it. But if anyone had looked at her mouth, they would have known she was lying.

$\mathcal{H}$e went back to the bar at the hotel, ordered a café con leche, and sat at a table in the corner by himself. He watched the people in the bar behave as if there was nothing wrong, drinking, smoking, laughing, the women dressed in brightly colored dresses, showing a bit more leg than was fashionable in New York. He thought about what Evangelina had said about her trip to Havana when she went to see General Weyler, "El Matador," as the Cubans called him. She did have a journalist's eye.

"It was such a strange experience," she had said, "as if I were in a dream-state, somewhere between waking and sleeping. The theaters and the concerts were going on, just the same as ever. The people in the streets were gay, gathering in the plaza to hear music, and it was hard to imagine that just beyond the gates, men were being tortured and women and small children were being killed for their beliefs. The Havana ladies are all very beautiful and they dress in gay, bright colors and soft, thin materials, which make them look like the flowers which grow so plentifully in every tiny garden there. There were parties and riding frolics and everywhere one saw the American tourists on their bicycles going out before breakfast to see where a battle had been fought. My sister Carmen made a joke that we should make up souvenirs and have a stand. The streets were full of swaggering, leering Spanish soldiers, some posted on the corners like sentries, but otherwise Havana seemed as peaceful as a convent garden; yet every day I read in the paper some little notice that on that morning So-and-So was executed for rebellion or disloyalty to the Spanish Government."

Mr. Hearst was right about her. She was the perfect story, an innocent with a conscience and the sensitivity of a woman much older than her years.

When he got up to his room, he looked at the package from the luggage shop. He untied the ribbon, opened the box, and took the paper off. It would, in any event, be an appropriate gift for Katherine. "A gift for a lady, nothing too intimate." He held it in his hand, the leather was terribly soft. He opened it and noticed a slip of paper sticking out from the billfold. Fool. He'd almost missed it. He unfolded the paper. Written on it, in blue pen, "The transport ship for Ceuta will leave in 10 days. You don't have much time."

*W*hen he saw her again, she looked frightened.

"I try," she said, "to hold on to my spirit . . ." She was very pale. She was gripping the table with both hands and the dress she had on was too small, cut in against the line of her shoulders, pressing her breasts, so that the curve of her bosom was visible above the bust-line, and it was frayed at the elbows so that her skin showed through. He wanted to take a shawl and put it around her shoulders and cover her.

"I try," she said, "to be one of those women who could walk the plank with no fear, to be an example. That is all that's left for me, is to be an example. If they send me to Africa, no one will ever hear from me again."

I will not let them send you to Ceuta, Evangelina. But he could not say this to her out loud.

"Will you write that in your paper, Mr. Duval? Will you tell them what my state of mind is? That I put up a valiant fight but that I lost?"

"I am hoping that will not be necessary."

He saw one of the guards start to approach them.

"They're watching us. Tell me about the first time you were in prison. When you went with your father to the Isle of Pines."

The guard was closer now.

"Is there any point?"

"Do exactly what I tell you. Tell me about the first time you were in prison."

She took a deep breath. "You know we were not imprisoned," she said, "my sister, Carmen, and I. It was our choice. We went to the Isle of Pines with my father so that we could take care of him." She stopped as if she were lost in thought.

"Continue, please."

"What does it matter if my story lives after me? What difference is my story from any of theirs. We will just become another one of the—disappeared. I woke this morning to a volley of gunfire from across in the square. Jailhouse rumour, 7 men were executed. I assume you could confirm that. We no longer believe in trial by jury. What does it matter if my story lives after me if none of us are here?"

"You will live to tell your story. Trust me, please.

They are watching us. Tell me about the Isle of Pines. Pull yourself together. Now."

"That seems odd to you, doesn't it? Not something an American woman would ever do. Choose to go to prison with her father."

"Not something an American woman would ever do," he agreed. Good girl. Keep talking. He thought about the notion that Katherine would accompany him to prison. He imagined her trying to decorate the cell, coordinate the menu. No, an American woman would not accompany her husband or her father to prison. "Rather," he said, "they would petition to get one out."

"I know about that," said Evangelina. She was referring, of course, to the many letters that had been written on her behalf by American women of a certain stature to Her Majesty María Cristina, Queen Regent of Spain, to His Holiness Pope Leo XIII, to no avail.

"An American woman," he went on, "would bring you fresh-baked bread, the latest novel, but I cannot imagine an American woman accompanying her father (or her husband) to prison."

If he went to prison would Katherine ever even know?

"Nor could I imagine," he added, "an American man allowing his wife or child to go to prison with him."

"Yes, in retrospect, I wonder why he let us do it." It was the first time she'd sounded at all bitter or derisive toward her father. "Perhaps," she said, softening her tone, "he thought we would be safer in prison with him."

The guards were on them then. Two of them. Looking over his shoulder to see his notes.

She smiled at them. She still had a rebel's spirit. She leaned in to speak to, as she knew him, Charles Duval. "It was not an easy journey to the Isle of Pines. One must travel across Cuba to Batabanó . . ."

He interrupted her. "Buenos días," he said to the guard.

The guard replied, "No se si es bueno o no." I do not know if it is a good day or not.

The guards moved on. "Continue, please. Make no remark. They are still watching us."

She did as she was told.

She had not yet seen him do anything dangerous or foolhardy, or draw attention to them in any way. He was not like Eugene Bryson who had been so vocal locally about her plight that she had not been surprised when the Spanish had evicted him from Cuba. She was starting to trust Charles Duval and admire him and, perhaps, think about him more than she ought to when she was alone.

"They put us in a train car made of steel," she said, "a 'travelling fort,' it's called, with many windows so that the soldiers can shoot out from it, if attacked. It was hot inside, stifling, like a sardine can and we were the sardines, the prisoners were bound together, and there were so many of us, it was not possible to sit.

Every time the train lurched, we were in danger of falling over on one another. It must have travelled very slowly for it took almost 8 hours to go the 35 miles to Batabanó.

"We were aware of the war around us. The bridge we were to cross had been blown up the day before, Maceo and his men. We should have taken pride in this but a train had turned over on its side. They told me not to look, but I couldn't help it. The train was badly burned and I saw what looked like charred bodies inside. We had done this. To what end? The bridge had been hastily repaired. It seemed unstable and I felt, as we crossed, as if it might collapse beneath the weight of the train and we might have a similar fate. I had, please do not write this, but I had lost heart. All I saw was death and destruction around me. My country had become a battleground. My father said, 'Do not forget, we fight for freedom.' But I had begun to wonder at what price.

"When we finally arrived at Batabanó, a seaport in the South, not pretty like the ones here, but dirty and dismal, where mostly the sponge fishermen stop, the steamer that was to take us had been loaded with a regiment of Spanish soldiers. They were after Maceo and they were hurrying as many troops as they could to fight him in the West. I prayed that none of our friends were with Maceo.

"We spent the night on the open wharf. The smell was enough to keep us awake. The sponge fishermen left their sponges in the sun to dry and they were piled high on the wharf, salty, acrid, like the, please do not think that I am unkind, like the smell of an old woman. Are you going to help me?"

He didn't think he'd heard her right. And she continued her story as if she hadn't digressed, at all.

"The next morning, the little steamer, the *Nuevo Cubano*, returned for us. The prisoners were still bound four abreast, had been made to sleep that way, and the soldiers with their loaded guns stood between us and the shore, to make sure that no one escaped. There was an inhumanity to the way that we were shoved onboard and made to sit in lines on the little boat that could barely contain us. It wasn't cold but there was a wind that blew steadily, the spray from the ocean hit our faces continuously. You haven't answered my question."

"Do you know if the guard has children?"

"Two."

"His name."

"Ernesto Herrara."

"Continue, please, with your story."

"As we neared the shore," her voice quavered, "I could see"—she was looking at him in a way she'd never looked at him before—"Santa Cruz, the harbor of the Isle of Pines. Its white-sand beach seemed to sparkle in the sunlight and it did not seem as if it were a prison, at all. It had been a tourist island until they took it over as a penal colony. We were housed in what had been a hotel, many, many years ago . . ." She laughed at that. "A mudhouse that had been divided in four parts."

He had to cut her off.

"We haven't much time, Evangelina."

"I've heard the rumours." There was an edge and a determination to her voice now. "Will you help me?"

"Yes. If you do exactly what I tell you to do."

"El Cañón de los Fantasmas. That is where my father is. Tell him that I miss him."

"Say no more. They're watching us. I want you to tell me about when you were arrested. Quickly, they're watching us. No, feign you have a headache. We'll start again tomorrow."

He had been up and down every side of the prison. In daylight and in the dead of night. It seemed an impenetrable fortress. No, not impenetrable. It was only two stories high, only a dozen kilometres from the other side of the street. Not impenetrable.

"Can you help me? Will you help me?" He heard her voice over in his mind and remembered how her eyes seemed filled with fear for the first time.

"Yes, Evangelina, I will help you." But he wondered if she knew there was a price.

$\mathcal{W}$hat if we don't find them?" said the young Cuban man to the other as they searched for Maceo and his men in the hills.

"We'll start our own . . ."

Every day there were more and more of them. For every man arrested, another fled to the mountains. For every child that was killed, another was stowed away in a little fishing village, vowing to take his father's place as soon as he was of age. If the Spanish thought that they could "put this down," they had miscalculated the deep-seated passion of the Cuban people, "Viva Cuba

Libre," and the avarice of the Americans' Manifest Destiny draped in a flag called democracy and freedom for all.

They had broken camp that morning. It was reported there were soldiers in the hills . . . looking for them. Guardia Civil and Spanish soldiers . . . The men were getting careless. Giddy. Unpredictable. From the crest of the mountain, Carlos could see the town below covered in a veil of mist. At least, they had fresh horses. And guns. And ammunition. Stolen the day before, by accident. Their best maneuvers had been by accident. It was when they planned things that they got in trouble. He fought with the old man about this. Evangelina's father thought everything should be planned (but where there was a plan, the details of it could be learned by others) and, witness yesterday's events, their best scores had been by accident. They had known about the horses but who would have guessed the two Spanish yahoos who were selling horses would also have a cache of weapons. The buyer? They'd asked them who the buyer was but when an answer had not been forthcoming, they had slit their throats, making any further conversation difficult.

The old man argued with that, how could they reconcile the violence? But the old man was naïve. They needed a place to set camp. Somewhere to rest for a few days. Somewhere hidden so that they would not have to move, like gypsies, before daybreak.

Time no longer had the same meaning that it had before. The year, which had been divided by weeks, months, marked by weddings, garden parties, birthdays, the school year stretching lazily to summer, planting, harvest, had now become an indistinguishable series of 24-hour periods in which the sun rose and set and there was something comforting and disconcerting about the night that covered them at the end of each day like a protective blanket.

They needed a place to set camp. The old man insisted there was a cave. Large, deep, hidden in the mountains. Well hidden, it appeared. Since none of the fissures or crevices in the rocky face of the mountain appeared to lead to it. There was a waterfall, its ice-blue water crystal clear, pristine, as though it were oblivious to the danger all around them. They stopped to drink from it, its water cool, refreshing, absolutely pure.

They heard horses' hooves approaching. Clipped. Faster. Men's voices, shouting to each other in hushed tones, seemingly a contradiction but the sound echoed in the mountains, its volume difficult to gauge, as well as its proximity. How many horses were there? How many horses' hooves . . . were they hearing echoes upon echoes, as if the sound were bouncing off one side of the mountain to the other and the echoes had a decibel of their own. Some people believed that the mountains held on to sound, on very quiet days one could still hear whispered conversations that had been had years before. The Cubans called it El Cañón de los Fantasmas (the Canyon of the Ghosts) and said that, in it, you could hear the voices of the ghosts. But these were real and fast approaching. Was it possible to make out the lilt of the accent? Were those Spanish voices or Cuban? And, if they were Cuban, whose side were they on?

They would take refuge in the densely wooded grove and pray that they could hold their silence. The old man still insisted there was a cave. If only they could find it before nightfall.

*W*hen he next saw her, she had regained her composure, at least on the surface, or else it was the calm of someone about to go on a suicide run. He was all business.

"Tell me about the Isle of Pines. Quickly, they're watching us."

She did as she was told. Her voice was measured. "Life there . . . ? You know, I have felt that way since this began, as if I am awake yet walking in my sleep, or else it is everyone else that is asleep. There we were on a perfectly beautiful island, prisoners, but safe in our exile or, at least, we thought we were safe. We had been told that my father would live there until the 'war' was over and then he would be released. (They called it a war already.) I was the one who started to have problems.

"A new military governor was appointed to run the Isle of Pines. He wasn't old, somewhere in his 20's, but arrogant. They said he was the nephew of the Minister of War in Cánovas del Castillo's Cabinet. That was, of course, how he got his job. From the moment he arrived, there was a tension to the prison that had never existed before; we felt, in some real way, like prisoners of war. General Weyler had appointed him. The rumour was that he was a coward and had asked to be governor of the Isle of Pines so that he would not have to fight in battle. I know he was a coward. Brave men do not act the way that he did. Brave men do not attack girls who do not carry swords.

"I remember the first time I saw Colonel Berriz. He was a short, ugly, dark man, with bushy hair and black whiskers on his cheeks. He looked a little bit like General Weyler except he had the most awful green eyes I've ever seen. Carmen and I called him 'Old green eyes.' He was walking with his secretary, Felix Sagrera. Felix was also a prisoner. He was a friend of my father's, from Cienfuegos, a revolutionary poet who, because of his literary skill, was made to 'work' for the governor. Many of the men from our village had been arrested and were imprisoned with us at the Isle of Pines, including Carlos."

She'd said so little to him about Carlos. Carlos Castell, who he knew was her intended, and whose reputation as a leading force in the revolution was becoming as much of a legend as hers.

She went on, "Felix Sagrera, my father's friend, came back to our house the next day. 'Evangelina,' he said, 'you have made a conquest. The governor is in love with you already.'

"I answered, 'Tell him he should keep his love.'

" 'Who am I to break a heart?' said Felix Sagrera. 'I will leave that part to you.' He made a joke of it. They all did, even my sister. Even Carlos. I was the only one who had a premonition it was serious.

"A few hours later, Colonel Berriz rode by the house alone on horseback. He stopped when he saw me outside and looked down at me. 'There is the prettiest little rebel of the war,' he said and then he rode on laughing.

"The next morning, he knocked on our door. 'Aren't you going to ask me in, Evangelina?' I was frightened. I was in the house alone but I did not want to be rude to him. He walked in and stood in the entryway of the little house. 'This is comfortable for a prison, is it not, Evangelina?'

"I replied politely. 'Yes, Colonel Berriz.' I was terrified that I would offend him.

" 'I try to make it as comfortable for my prisoners as I can, but from you, I see no gratitude. I hate to lock people up,' he said, 'it wounds me to my very soul. But is a governor to be the only one who suffers?'

" 'I hear my father calling me,' I said, even though there was no one home but me. 'I must go.' I held the door open for him and he left and I could hear him laughing again as he rode away.

"The next day, two prison guards arrived at our door. They handcuffed my father and took him away. They ransacked the little house. They had no warrant. And when I asked them what the charges were against my father, they said, 'It is difficult to say, as yet.' He was put in the restricted part of the prison, in a solitary cell in the 'jail for exiles.' I went immediately to Berriz' office. 'Why is my father arrested, Colonel Berriz?' I asked as soon as I'd been led in the door.

" 'What difference why?' he shrugged. 'When he has such a beautiful daughter to intercede for him. He is no longer under arrest.' He snapped his fingers and directed one of the guards to release my father. 'You see,' he said, 'I can refuse you nothing. You will come to me again tomorrow and I will see how grateful you are.'

"Of course, I did not go to him. And we heard nothing for three days. I told my father all that had happened and he gave me a dagger to keep in the sleeve of my dress. The next morning, my father was arrested again.

"That night, I saw out the window a shadow and then it moved from the wall. The moonlight touched it and glittering spots appeared all over it. It moved closer and I saw it was a man. And then, again, he was swallowed in the shadow of the wall. I took the dagger and hid it in the sleeve of my dress. All night, I had felt as if there was something dark coming, as if I had a chill.

I cannot explain exactly how. But when you pray and tell your beads and no answer comes from Heaven, and instead you get a shiver that seems to come from inside. My nurse used to tell me that this was the shadow of the dark angel's wing on one's soul."

He interrupted her, "I know what that feels like."

"I thought you might . . .

"Soon the man appeared from the shadows again. He had put his full uniform on, the glitter was from the gold lace on his shoulders and cap, from the stars on his collar, from the braid on his breast and the hilt of his sword that appeared just above his belt. He jumped up on the veranda, swinging himself effortlessly over the bannister. It was Colonel Berriz. He had put on his finery and his military stripes. He knocked on my door. When I didn't answer, he kicked the door in."

"There are those who say you lured him to your room."

"That is not the truth, Mr. Duval—but I knew that he would come . . .

"I begged him not to molest me. To treat my father as he would any other prisoner . . .

"Berriz laughed at me and said he had not come dressed for court, he made a pun that surprised me, just to hear a rebel's lecture.

"He caught me by the wrist. He said he loved me and tried to lift my hand to his lips. When I resisted, he said that it was dangerous for me to argue with him and he ripped my dress. And very softly, he said, as he looked down on me, 'I love you better than anything in the world.'

"I knew he did not speak the truth. No one who loved that way would want to hurt the one they love. I tried to run past him. He caught me by the shoulders and pushed me against the wall. I was too frightened to cry out. I did not let my eyes leave his, I did not want him to know that I was frightened. My sister Carmen was asleep in the next room. I prayed she would not wake up and try to help me. I feared that if he had a witness, neither of us would survive. Colonel Berriz tried to kiss me. He shook me by the shoulders and, all the time, kept crying out my name, over and over again, and saying that he loved me. He tried to kiss me again but not on my mouth this time and that was when I pulled the dagger. I got him on the shoulder and then he grabbed my wrist and wrenched the knife from me and that was when I screamed.

"It happened so quickly. That was when the others came. Dozens of men from the other houses like ours. I dare not say their names. In a moment, they had Berriz to the ground. They had tied a bandanna in his mouth to muffle his cries. I stood and watched them defend my honour and all I said was, 'Do you want a lecture from a Cuban rebel now?' "

*W*hat part of this would Katherine understand . . . ?

That he was part of something much bigger than himself.

That he had taken this assignment and, no matter what the risk was to himself, he would try to successfully accomplish it.

That he was falling in love with her . . .

Her eyes had flashed when she had said that last bit, "Would you like a lecture from a Cuban rebel now?"

It was her spirit he was attracted to and the notion that he would be able to save her. But after that, would he always want to keep her safe. Everything about this was starting to feel dangerous and complicated.

If he could only have bribed one of the guards . . . Eduardo Cortez had one of his men approach Ernesto Herrara, the guard who had been lurking. Turned down flat. If it had been anyone else except Evangelina Cisneros, no problem. But she was too high profile, the risk was too high. They dared not approach anyone else. For if they were turned down again, then the guards would have been aware that there were plans afoot. Plans . . . as yet, he could see no clear means of escape. She was starting to believe in him.

It was her spirit he was falling in love with. Hold on to your spirit, Evangelina, or I will not be able to help you.

"That was when they arrested you?"

"No, not just then . . . In the chaos that ensued, Carlos, my father, and I escaped the prison. We hid on the island for three days . . . but they came after us. When it was clear that we were surrounded, I had to make a choice.

"I knew that it was me they wanted, that I would be enough for them, that I could distract them long enough for my father and Carlos to get away.

"I turned to Carlos. 'Go. Now. Quickly. Save my father. You will see me again. I promise. Go. Quickly.' He leaned in, for one brief moment, and kissed me. And, as he and my father fled for the perimeter of the island, I stepped out from the brush.

"Colonel Berriz was facing me, surrounded by his men. He held a gun on me. And all I could say was, 'Would you shoot someone you love so well?'

"That was when I was arrested. Charged with an insurgence. They said that there had been an uprising. That there were cries of 'Viva Cuba Libre.' That I had lured Colonel Berriz to my house so the others could attack him. That there had been shots fired. But none of us had guns. You know the rest, I think."

"I have always wondered," he said, watching her so that he could gauge her reaction, "how your father and Carlos escaped from the island."

She smiled slightly. "They took a boat."

"You make it seem so benign. Tell me, can you run a war from prison?"

She smiled at him. "I don't know about a war," she said, "but possibly an uprising. It depends on what prison you're in. You look tired, Mr. Duval. Did you not sleep well last night?"

"I was up quite late, reading about the architecture of prisons."

She waited a moment and then very softly said, "You need my help, don't you? You don't know how to get me out."

He didn't answer but his silence was an answer in itself.

"I trust you, Mr. Duval. Do you trust me?" She didn't wait for him to answer her. "Write a story about me tonight in your notebook that is unflattering. That it is your opinion that I led an insurgence, that I brought this sentence on myself. Then, come back tomorrow, and turn your notebook toward me so that I may read it. God be with you."

"God be with us both," he thought, but he did not say this out loud. Out loud, he said, "Your father sends his love."

Dear Katherine,

But he could get no further with the letter than the date and the salutation. What good was writing a letter that he could not send, that he had no means to send? And if he could have figured out a way to post it, what would he have said to her . . . Described the scenery when he couldn't even tell her where he was? The white sand beaches edged with palm trees. The baroque, colonial architecture of the elegant hotels. The open, smiling faces of the Cuban natives whose eyes were marred with fear and sorrow. Told her that he was frightened? He wasn't frightened, exhilarated perhaps, the way one is before a race begins, but he would not have been able to admit that or recognize it. Told her that he was involved with the most dangerous, foolhardy enterprise he'd ever attempted and that he did not know what the result of it would be or if he would ever see her again. But he did not want to allow himself those thoughts or think about that possibility. Told her that he missed her. Told her that he was falling in love with someone else.

He sat down to write the story as Evangelina had instructed him. The version where she was not an innocent. *She was not an innocent.* The version where she was not a pawn. *She was a pawn in a bigger game than she even knew.* It was not a story Mr. Hearst would ever run and he would have some trouble composing it so that it seemed as though he were writing his true convictions and yet he was surprised how easy it was to paint a different picture of her.

Havana was a city that never slept and when he went to bed at three, there was still the incongruous sound of music and laughter from the streets.

This would be the last time he would spend enough time in the prison yard to study it, he knew every impenetrable corner by heart. It was a God forsaken place . . .

He would not let them send her to Africa.

. . . The midday sun was high in the air, the smell of human excrement almost unbearable. Barely fit for animals. Let alone a home for women. Let alone a home for Evangelina. And yet compared to Ceuta, it would seem a palace.

He would not let them send her to Ceuta.

It was no longer about doing a job he had been hired to do. He didn't know how it was going to be possible, but he would break her out of the *Casa de Recojidas* the next night.

He looked around the prison yard. As simple as its construction was, three walls around a prison yard, the fourth being the prison itself, it was strangely impenetrable, like an ancient stone fortress. The cell windows were barred, the finest iron (sold to them by the Americans), the corridor windows were barred, and all were in plain view of the guards posted like sentries on the walls of the parapet. The worst problem was not within the prison itself. Directly behind it was the arsenal where presently were housed 462 Spanish troops, give or take a few on any given night, ready to mobilize at the least sign of trouble.

Where was Evangelina? Why weren't they bringing her to him?

And then he saw her. She looked very tiny as she walked toward him, flanked on both sides by Spanish guards, each of whom was carrying a rifle.

"Buenos días," he said to the one guard. The answer was the same as always, "No se si es bueno o no." I do not know if it is a good day or not.

The guards waited until she was seated and then left them alone, if you could call their exposed position, in plain sight of the guards and other inmates, alone. He prayed that this would not be the last time they would be alone together. That they would one day really be alone.

"I have broken my rule and written something down," she said. "There are three clues in it. You must find all three. Now, do exactly as I tell you. Pretend you are writing something. No, don't pretend, actually write something. Now, turn the notebook to me as if you want me to read it."

She must have practiced many times, taking the small folded paper from her sleeve. He barely saw her slip it between the pages of his notebook as she held the top page up, as if she were studying his words. "Don't worry—if anyone finds it, they will think I am simply being romantic and young and dark. No competition for José Martí. Anyone in my position could have written something similar." For a moment, her eyes seemed flat, as if they had lost their usual spark. "May God be with you."

This time, he said it out loud, "May God be with us both."

"Have you ever acted, Mr. Duval?"

He nodded. Didn't she know that he was acting now?

"Please follow my lead."

She seemed to study the words in his notebook and her eyes flashed darkly. "How could you write this about me?!" she screamed, not caring if anyone could hear her. She wanted them to hear her. She turned the notebook back to him. "Haven't you listened to anything I've said?" She spit this last. "Traitor!" She pushed her chair back from the table and stood up. "Guards! Guards!" she called. "Please, I wish to be taken back to my cell."

Damn her. It was a wild miscalculation. Two guards were on her immediately. And then another two seized him. He heard an unmistakable sound as the guards who were posted sentry on the parapet cocked and aimed their rifles.

"Where are you taking me? I've done nothing wrong!" They confiscated his notebook and his pen, the pen that Katherine had given him when they were still engaged, the first Christmas that they were together, which he had always felt held luck for him.

They escorted him outside the prison and let him go. They did not return his notebook or his pen.

$\mathcal{H}$e walked back to the Hotel Inglaterra and, after ordering dinner to be sent up later in the evening, went straight to his room. He busied himself reading and writing, trying to reconstruct the article that had been taken from him. Better to appear as normal as he could.

He barely picked at his food when it arrived, allowing himself a bit of soup, some bread, a half a glass of red wine. At 9:30, as expected, there was a sharp knock on his door. Two Spanish soldiers in the hallway. "You are to come with us, Sir," the younger of the soldiers said.

The other one, who appeared to be a captain, asked, "What is that you are writing, Sir?"

"I am trying to reconstruct the article that was taken from me. Whatever else, I must file a story."

They confiscated the new draft, as well. He'd expected that.

"You are to come with us, Sir," the younger one said again.

"Of course. A moment while I put my boots on."

They left the door to the room open so anyone passing in the hall could see that they were waiting for him. Would this cause problems for him later, bring him a certain notoriety so that his comings and goings would be noticed.

The soldiers escorted him down the front stairs into the lobby. He did his best to appear as though he were fraternizing with them, rather than being escorted by them out.

Where? Where were they taking him?

They closed him into a military carriage. The soldiers rode in front. He rode in back and did his best to appear as though he were not a prisoner, rather someone important enough to have a military escort.

They stopped in front of the Palace. They were taking him to be interrogated. He could have guessed that. The question was, were they planning to release him? Were they planning to incarcerate him? Were they planning to exile him as they had done Eugene Bryson? Hearst would not be thrilled if that was the outcome of this.

They led him up the steps of the Palace and up the marble staircase to the second floor. They left him in the richly appointed waiting room, Aubusson carpets on the floor, tapestries on the wall, and a bust of Queen Isabella on the marble-topped credenza. The velvet couch was strangely uncomfortable, big Spanish furniture with wooden bench-like backs.

After a terribly long time, the big double doors to one of the suites opened. Another soldier, in slightly more formal dress. "General Weyler will see you now." So, it was Weyler who would interrogate him. There would be no second chances. He felt as though he was about to be on point.

Weyler did not get up from his desk, barely looked up from his papers when he entered. There were three soldiers posted inside the door who did not leave the room.

"Your reputation precedes you, Sir."

As does yours. But he dared not say this out loud.

"Am I to believe this piece of yours?"

"I told Miss Cisneros that I would only print the truth."

"Your Mr. Hearst is not of the same school as you, I am afraid."

"He has never edited me before." He knew that Julian Hawthorne would never run this piece. They had a special encryption—quite simply "Eyes Only" at the top left margin—that meant the article had been written under some kind of duress and was not for publication. He studied Weyler. "She was not as innocent as my predecessor would have had us believe."

"No, nor was her family. But you probably do not approve of our decision to send her to Africa."

"It does not matter what I approve of. I was not appointed judge in this matter."

"I hope, for your sake, you mean that. You may not believe this, but we would prefer a peaceful, solution to all of this. We would prefer not to be heading toward certain war. You think, because I am a general, that it is war that would interest me. But a peaceful solution is not possible unless we remove her kind." He passed him the notebook back. Almost safe.

"When were you planning to run this story?"

"When will you send her away?"

"I cannot tell you that. I would ask you not to print her poem. It is sad, romantic, young, dark." As she had predicted.

"May I see her one more time?"

"She is very beautiful, is she not? I remember when I first met her. She came to ask for leniency for her father. I granted it. I felt then that they were more dangerous dead than alive. The legacy of José Martí. That in death, they become mythologized. Martyrs. But, I no longer feel that way. Of course you may. I have never denied you access to her."

He passed him back the poem. Really, almost safe now.

It made him bold. "My pen? Did you perhaps mean to return that, as well."

"I did not know we had taken a pen from you."

"A fountain pen. It was a gift from my wife."

"I did not know you had a wife."

His mind flipped to Duval's biography. Had he made a mistake? Almost. Not exactly.

"Yes, a wife and two daughters. But their mother, my wife, is no longer living. Making the gift all the more precious to me."

"And you never remarried?"

"No, not yet."

"Your daughters must mind, then, having you away."

"I think it is harder on me."

Weyler looked across at one of the soldiers by the

door. "May I offer you a drink, Mr. Duval. A cigar?"

"A lemonade if you have one."

"You may not believe this, but we prefer a peaceful solution."

Weyler walked across to the bar. He was a shorter man than he had appeared sitting down, not attractive, dark piercing eyes that were difficult to read. Weyler poured himself a whiskey which he barely diluted with a splash of water.

Duval looked across at the soldiers guarding the door, each with a sword in the sheath of his belt and a rifle at his side. He, too, hoped a peaceful solution would be possible.

"Yes, I believe it. Bloodshed is never limited to one side."

"When a hundred people call themselves a nation," said General Weyler, "it is easy to ignore. But there are thousands of them. The planters are under their control now, the plantation owners are frightened of them. None of this is for attribution. The peasants in the seaside villages harbor them, not realizing what they do. Was it your Mr. McKinley who said, 'They are too primitive to govern themselves.' "

"No, it was J. C. Breckenridge, the Under-Secretary of War."

"I have been remiss, Mr. Duval. I should have invited you for a drink when you first arrived."

"No. I should have asked for an audience with you."

"Audience . . . the Palace was not my choice. But it

allows a safe surrounding in a city, a country about to go mad."

"Let's hope that that is not the case." The lemonade was lukewarm, bitter. He forced himself to take another sip.

"She is not important. And yet you continue to write about her."

"She is good copy."

"She is not as innocent as she seems."

"Yes, I am aware of that."

"She is very beautiful."

"If you like terribly young women."

"Have we hit on a cultural difference? Somehow, I doubt that." Weyler opened the drawer of his desk. He took out the fountain pen, black, slightly edged with gold. "Is this your pen, Mr. Duval? They must have given it to me by mistake."

He'd had it all along. He slid the fountain pen across the desk.

"Yes, it is." Almost safe. "Thank you. Am I free to go?"

"You were always free to go."

*E*vangelina's poem . . .

It was written in very careful script and, at the top, she had written, "If I were to title it, I would call it, 'Longing.'"

> If my tears were like rain and they could wash
>   away the sorrow . . .
> But they have grown bitter, acidic, not strong
>   enough to break the bars . . .
> I dream of a window on the courtyard, looking
>   out on the tiled fountain of my youth,
> where the water, flecked with turquoise, seemed
>   to dance in the sun.

92

If my sleep could drown the cries of the others
Like morphine sleep, filled with dreams and
    memories . . .
But it is restless, dreamless,
the sleep of the dead, or the soon to be dead.

If my tears were like rain and they could wash
    away the sorrow
but they have grown bitter, acidic, not strong
    enough to break the bars
and I lie here restless, longing for sleep, the sleep
    of the dead
or the soon to be dead, anything to set me free.

He remembered her words. "Study it. In it, you will
find three clues. You must find all of them."

The first was easy—acid, to melt the bars. But how
to get it to her . . .

The second was also easily discernible—morphine, to
put her cellmates to sleep. Easier to pass a small packet
of morphine.

And the third . . . Was there a window that he did not
know about? A window that looked down on a courtyard in which there was a fountain through which he
could secure her release . . . ?

Study it.

The two things she'd requested were easily procured. Was there anything Eduardo Cortez couldn't get? The morphine which had been carefully injected into chocolates. Three glass vials of sulphuric acid secured by cork stoppers and sealed with wax. He would pass her only one. Three would be too difficult to give her. How to pass her any of it? He would take her hand. He had wanted to for some time. And she would hide it in the sleeve of her dress and walk back carefully to her cell so that it would not fall to the floor.

∾

The atmosphere in the prison yard was hostile. Three Negro women had been involved in a fight that morning with a Cuban girl. One of them had pulled a knife and sliced the Cuban girl on the side of her face. The three Negroes had been taken away in chains. The Cuban girl had been taken to the infirmary. The prison had divided into factions and there was a tension in the air as if at any moment, another altercation could break out.

He sat at the little table in the center of the prison yard, feeling exposed, and vulnerable. After what seemed a terribly long time, Ernesto Herrara came out to the prison yard and walked over to the table.

"She has refused to see you. We could force her, of course, but a public display would not be good for the morale of the other prisoners. Don't you agree?"

How could that be true? Why would she refuse to see him . . . Were they keeping her in isolation and making it seem as if it were her choice? Better not to press.

"Of course. I understand. She must have said everything she chooses to. Buenos días."

And the answer was the same as always, "No se si es bueno o no."

As he started to leave the prison, he noticed the largest of the black women, Nadine, looking at him. She put her fingers up to her mouth and made as if she were about to whistle. He did not know if that was a sign of anything, at all.

When he returned to the hotel, the heavy-set man, the one he'd ascertained was most likely an officer in the Guardia Civil, who had been practically his shadow since he'd arrived in Havana, was settled into a rattan sofa in the lobby, smoking a cigar. "Charles Duval" made the peculiar decision to sit down across from him and read the morning paper. His reasoning being that it would be better not to appear skittish or to let on that he was on to him. He considered, for a moment, engaging him in conversation but that would perhaps be too bold. He remembered from his training: It is always near the end that one has the tendency to be careless.

The big French doors in the lobby were open to the patio and the already languid pace of the hotel was slowed even more by the warm breeze blowing in from the garden, fragrant with the smell of tropical flowers and the sea. He ordered a café con leche to be served to him in the lobby and settled in to wait.

Criss-crossed patterns of sunlight fell across the faded carpet. There was an arrangement of lilies and birds of paradise, the lilies pale white, the birds of paradise azure blue and orange, in a ceramic vase on the coffee table. An old man was asleep in the chair in the corner, his trousers held up by suspenders that gaped as he slouched over in his sleep. Tomorrow, someone else would sit here and read the paper. If all went well, "Charles Duval" would no longer be a resident of the hotel. He overtipped the boy who brought him the coffee and wondered if he had a sister at home or an older brother who had joined the revolutionary party. He drank the café con leche, its rich flavor barely tempered by the warm milk. When he looked up from the newspaper, his "shadow" was gone, and there was only the old man sitting in the chair in the corner, asleep.

He left the newspaper on the table and walked slowly and pointedly to the desk to collect his key and messages, in the event he was still being observed. There was an invitation to lunch the following Tuesday from the wife of a fellow journalist which he wouldn't bother to decline.

He took the stairs up to the second floor and then the third. He walked down the hall, slowly, to his room. When he put the key in the lock, the door swung open, unlocked, unlatched. He knew he had secured it when he'd left. He reached for the pistol he had tucked into the waist of his trousers that morning.

He stood in the open doorway of the room, for a moment . . . and could see, through the bathroom door, the maid on her hands and knees scrubbing the tiled floor of the bathroom. She was a tiny creature with long dark hair done up in a bun and she looked at him with big eyes as though she were equally as surprised to see him, or rather the gun that he was now holding in his hand.

The room was still in a state of disarray, as he had left it, the bed unmade, a sheaf of papers that he'd scattered on the desk to make it appear as if he were in the midst of writing something. Everything seemed to still be in its place.

"Un momentito, Señor," she said from the floor.

He put the gun away. "Perhaps it would be better if I came back."

Her actions surprised him. She rose and moved across the room, quickly, shutting the door behind him, turning the lock.

"Yo soy la esposa de Ernesto Herrara." I am the wife of Ernesto Herrara.

Ernesto Herrara. The guard at the prison.

"Perhaps it would be best if you stayed." She looked

at him again with very big eyes. Her voice was soft, melodic. "I have many children, Señor."

He knew she had only two.

"I have need for extra work." He understood from this that she had need of money. Who didn't, besides Mr. Hearst? "I was told you might have extra work for me."

"And what sort of work did you have in mind to do?"

"I can do many things, Señor."

"Who told you about this position?"

"It is not important who I learned this from."

They were being very careful with each other. It was clear that she was frightened, anyway. And, for Decker, one precipitous move could mean that it was over.

She began to dust the bedside table so that it would appear as if she were cleaning as she continued, "I do not do this only for money, Señor. I do this because she would do the same for me. None of us want her to be sent to Ceuta. Be quick. I do not wish to spend much time with you." She put her fingers to her lips and made as if she were about to whistle and he knew that it was Evangelina who had arranged this meeting. He was duly impressed. Evangelina took direction well. She was resourceful. He hoped that those qualities would not be needed in the next few days but, if they were, he was glad that she possessed them. He remembered her words, "Do you trust me, Mr. Duval? I trust you."

Yes, I trust you, Evangelina. And, I hope, when this is all over, that you will still have the occasion to trust me.

La esposa de Ernesto Herrara was getting nervous. "Rápido."

He took the small box of chocolates from his pocket. Each piece wrapped in quilted paper.

He handed her the box. "Make sure your children do not find them and think they are dessert. The morphine in them is quite strong. Tell Evangelina to ration them, give no one more than one. I do not want to be responsible for putting someone into a sleep they have difficulty coming out of. I hope I am not putting you in danger."

"It is all dangerous, Señor. That is why it is expensive."

He took a small gold cross and chain from his pocket. He held it up to the light.

"This cross is for her to hang in the window as a signal to let us know that all is well. It's inset with diamonds, which should catch the moonlight. If we do not see it hanging there, we will leave."

He said a prayer as he wrapped it gingerly in the tissue from the luggage shop. May God be with you, Evangelina. He put the cross in the small box and laid the leather wallet on top of it. It would not be a present for Katherine, after all.

He handed her that little box, as well.

"I have put some money in the wallet," he said. "The bills are old and in small denominations. I hope you use it well for your children."

"Gracias, Señor. You must leave, now, Señor, and let me finish my work. Buenos días."

He did not answer her the way her husband always answered him. "Buenos días, Señora," he said and, stopping briefly to get his hat, left her in the hotel room alone.

*E*duardo Cortez was seated at a table with two very beautiful women, one of them the girl he had pointed out to Karl Decker when they had first met in the cafe.

Decker had checked her background, her name was Ana Maria Varona, although even if he hadn't, he would have been able to make her history up. She was from the small village of Las Tunas where she had lived since she was a little girl. Her father, one of Maceo's men, had been killed by Spanish assailants, in the same skirmish in which Maceo was wounded.

Shortly after her father's death, the Spanish came to the little house she was raised in, on a Sunday morning, as they were just preparing to go to church. Ana Maria watched as her mother and brothers were arrested. She found her mother's prayer shawl in the dirt outside their house. In order to set an example, her brothers were publicly executed the next morning in the square. Her mother's whereabouts? Unknown. They had not arrested Ana Maria and she had never understood why.

He remembered Eduardo's words. "She doesn't work for money. We will pay her but that is not why she is here. Which one of us do you trust more? I'll answer for you," he said. "Me, because I am not willing to die."

"But . . . ," thought Decker, "there might be times when one would rather trust one's life to someone who is willing to die."

The restaurant was crowded. As had been previously arranged, he walked along the waterfront, appearing to wander, by chance into *El Pescado,* the outdoor cafe and fish market at the edge of the dock, for lunch. He sat at a table alone in the middle of the restaurant. As he had been instructed, he had taken with him the slim volume of Rubén Darío poetry which he left open, face-down on the table, as if he were in the midst of reading it.

"If it's to go, leave the book open, if we are to be delayed, leave the slim volume closed on the table. We may not have a chance to speak again until this is over. Remember, what I told you—trust no one."

He ordered a glass of wine, a Spanish madeira, and a plate of grilled lobster. Might as well enjoy what food they had to offer. God knew there would be no sitting in outdoor cafes tomorrow.

They would go that night. And, if they were successful, remain in hiding for a few days before finding passage home. If all went well. And, if all did not go well, God knew where he would be tomorrow.

Ana Maria got up from the table and began to walk toward him. For a moment their eyes met and he saw something besides determination in her eyes.

He made as if he were a coarse American staring at a Cuban girl. She smiled back at him suggestively. But, as she approached him, he sensed the atmosphere in the cafe had changed, as if people had stopped speaking in mid-sentence, and many of them were holding their breath. She began to walk more slowly as a voice behind him said, "Are you a fan of modernismo?"

He turned and saw General Valeriano Weyler standing behind him. "I have not read much of Rubén Darío, to tell the truth," he replied, "but I would have imagined that you would find his work too subversive."

Weyler laughed. "Sometimes one makes excuse for substance," he said, "when the form is so extraordinary."

"I am surprised to hear you say that."

"If you knew me better, Mr. Duval, many things about me would surprise you." He picked up the slim volume of Rubén Darío's poems and looked at it, reading a few lines from the page to which it was open. Then, he shut the book and set it down on the table.

"Oh, I'm so sorry," he said, "I seem to have lost your place," as Ana Maria reached the table and noted, incorrectly, the position of the book.

"Are you still staying at the Inglaterra?"

"Yes, I like it there," said Decker modulating his tone so that it would not betray any emotion. A frightened waiter set a plate of lobster in front of him, its bright red claws upturned and closed as if it had tried to strike at something.

"Your food has arrived," said General Weyler. "I do not wish to disturb you, but we must someday arrange to have lunch together."

"If it would please you," said Karl Decker, hoping that possibility would never occur.

He watched as General Valeriano Weyler walked through the crowded restaurant and exited onto the dock. The atmosphere in the cafe lightened considerably. He cracked open a lobster claw, took a small bite of the meat, then opened the slim volume of poetry again, glanced at the page, as if finding his place, and laid it, once more, open on the table. But when he looked over to where Eduardo Cortez had been sitting, in the company of the two Cuban girls, there was no one there, at all.

"The first day you met me," she thought to herself, "I'd fallen in the creek. I was wearing a blue gingham bathing costume that had been my sister's. I'd skinned my knee. My pigtails were wet. And I was crying." Out loud she said, "Sandy will want to see you." Sanderson Warren Hanover III was Betsy's husband, Sandy to his friends, plantation owner, sugar baron, with family interests that extended to Cuba and Hawaii. Decker had heard that they were living here. How could he get them to go along with this charade.

"You're awfully naughty," said Betsy, "not to have sent us a message and let us know you were in Havana."

"I wasn't certain you were here. It's been so long since I've seen you." He got very formal. "There's been so little time. But I would be pleased if you introduced me to your husband."

He whispered in her ear, "Do you think you can pull this off?"

She looked at him almost challengingly. "Yes, dear. Can you?"

They were drinking sloe gin fizzes (in that way that Americans have of bringing their culture with them wherever they go). The atmosphere was raucous and genteel, as if those two things weren't a contradiction. Yes, the rumours were flying that Weyler was about to be recalled, fueled by the fact that, curiously, there were no Spanish officers in the room. But even if the rumours were true, there was not time enough for it to have any effect on Evangelina Cisneros—the transport ship for Ceuta was leaving in six days, a message would not even arrive from Spain by then . . . and no guarantee that it would alter her fate, at all. She was an embarrassment, best to send her away. The only recourse would be to successfully break her out of prison. Damn. What he did not want was to be trapped inside the Hotel Inglaterra. There was too much to be done. And now, it would require diplomacy to extricate himself from the Hanovers' company. Best not to appear rude. Better to have a drink with them and accrue the beginnings of an alibi for the evening.

He didn't know what Betsy Hanover had said to her husband, but they had played their parts flawlessly . . . And he had, for a moment, relaxed even, in his effort to appear normal. But without his asking, they had placed another drink before him, the soup had been served, the entrees were about to arrive, it was almost nine-thirty, and he needed to excuse himself gracefully from their table. There was no contingency for the others to "go" without him. He hoped everything had been carefully set in motion. That they would have gathered at the house on O'Farrill Street. The carriage driver would be waiting, two blocks away from the *Casa de Recojidas*. Another carriage driver by the docks. The back door to someone's kitchen had been left open and upstairs a guest room with the bed turned down was waiting for her, a candle burning, and a light supper on a tray on the bedside table. He would take the second carriage and by the time it reached its destination, "Charles Duval" would have disappeared and "Peter Chelsohm," a cotton grower from Atlanta, would have taken his place with the aid of another passport given him by Mr. Hawthorne. *If . . . assuming . . . if . . . they could break her out. And assuming they had correctly interpreted his signal that afternoon which he had no way of knowing.*

$\mathcal{H}$ernandon, Pedro, and Miguel were playing poker. The door to the little house was open and a pile of wooden matches was visible in the center of the table. Hernandon was losing. He'd had no cards all evening and hoped it wasn't a precursor of what his luck would be for the rest of the night. It was getting late and there was still no sign of the American. Miguel put a bottle of cognac and three glasses on the table. Against his better judgment, Hernandon poured himself a shot. They heard footsteps approaching . . . and then there was a police officer in the doorway, his gaudy red and blue uniform, a bright patch of color against the gray Havana night. His boots heavy, his sword evident and large at his side.

Gambling was illegal in Havana. "I'm sure you'll tell me you play only for sport," said the officer.

"What fun is it to play if you have nothing to lose," said Hernandon. "We play for matches." He offered the policeman a shot of cognac.

"I never drink when I'm working," said the officer.

"Perhaps a hand or two with us?"

"I am afraid," said the officer, "that your matches are more than I can afford. Buenas noches."

The three men scarcely breathed until they were certain his footsteps had receded into the distance. "Why did you do that?" said Pedro.

"I did not want to seem as if I wanted to get rid of him. That would have made him suspicious. He would not arrest three Cuban men for a little betting. Besides," he laughed, "he seemed an easy mark and my luck being what it is tonight . . ."

Miguel laughed but Pedro, who was the most serious of the three, was not of a mind to find anything amusing. It was almost ten-thirty and still no sign of the American journalist. The clouds were starting to break in the sky and they would not have the benefit of a moonless night.

Hernandon lit a cigar and slipped out the back door ostensibly to be certain, as had been arranged, a carriage waited two blocks away on Egido Street. The guards on the parapet were armed with rifles and just beyond the jail, in the arsenal, 300 soldiers were asleep. They were half-mad to attempt this and no one should be surprised when it failed. He found the driver sitting in the carriage, already looking weary of being at his post.

"I brought you a cigar," said Hernandon. He walked with the man, around the corner, to the entrance of the alley. He reached into his jacket pocket to hand him a cigar and came out with a large hunting knife and neatly slit the driver's throat.

Inside the little house, Pedro put a pot of coffee up. They needed their wits about them. He put a sweet bread on the table. And when Hernandon returned and took his place at the table, assuring them the driver and the carriage were in place, it did not occur to them to question him. Pedro dealt another poker hand, five-card draw, nothing wild. Hernandon moaned when he saw his cards.

Miguel laughed. "If I could tell our fortune by this hand," he said, "I would say that we are going to be very lucky."

"You're bluffing," said Pedro.

"Am I . . . four matches says I'm not."

'I'll see your four," said Pedro who was holding aces and queens, "and raise you one."

"Four kings," said Miguel as he put his cards down on the table.

And then a voice behind them said, "Gentlemen, I hope our luck holds."

Without turning around, Hernandon said, "We did not know if you were coming."

"We are the same, then. I did not know," said Karl Decker, "if you would be here to meet me."

*H*e was relieved when he had seen that the front door to the little house on O'Farrill Street was open, a half-empty bottle of cognac on the table which he hoped was merely a prop. So far, so good. He took his place at the table. Pedro poured him a cup of coffee. Miguel counted out a small pile of matches and pushed it across the table to him. He proceeded to win three hands.

Hernandon said softly, "Are you certain you were not followed?"

"Fairly certain. I did my best not to be."

He had left the Hotel Inglaterra by the front lobby door and walked through the square, pointedly, as if he were trying to draw attention to himself, being so bold as to whistle a bit when he walked. He trusted his Cuban "shadow" was behind him somewhere and hoped this slight departure would throw him off. At No. 8 Bernaza Street, he opened the iron, grillwork gates and let himself into the courtyard. He walked up a flight of stairs, noisily, two at a time, the heels of his boots clicking noisily as he hit each terra cotta stair. He rang the bell of No. 21, the front apartment on the second floor.

Her name was Alicia. He did not know anything more about her. She opened the door, barefoot, wearing a simple cotton skirt and blouse that clung suggestively to her form. Her hair was down. She appeared to be in her 20's. She was very beautiful and smelled of the carnation water that was the rage among young Cuban women. He pushed past her into the apartment and she shut the door behind him.

"It was so late," she whispered. "I did not know if you were coming."

"How could I stay away?" he said, in character, as if this were an assignation.

She moved quickly across the room and turned the gaslight up on the wall sconce, so that the room was slightly more illuminated. She walked over to the front window and stood there with her back to him. He walked up behind her and put his arms around her waist and began to kiss her neck. She arched her back into him. In full view in the window, he took his hands and lightly ran them up along her body to her breasts. She arched her back again. She turned and let him kiss her. She took his hand and led him away from the window through the apartment to the bedroom.

Once inside, she closed the bedroom door and, without hesitation, moved quickly across the room. A curtain, hung behind the bed, draped slightly over the wall, as if it were a decoration. She pulled the heavy velvet curtain aside and visible in the wall was a hole that had been cut there that led to the apartment next door.

"I am sorry we do not have more time together," said "Charles Duval."

She kissed him softly on his cheek and whispered in his ear, "Viva Cuba Libre."

*H*eavy curtains had been drawn shut across the windows. Two men were speaking to each other, rapidly, in Spanish. Karl Decker was forcibly pulled into the room. He heard the sound of a heavy chest as it was dragged across the floor and pushed back against the wall. The apartment was dimly lit by candles and before he could adjust to the faint light and see clearly, a scarf was thrown before his eyes and tied behind his head. Almost as if it were a reflex, with the precision of some-one who had been trained, even though he did not have the use of his eyes, with his left hand, he grabbed the man who had tied him by the back of the neck and with his right, drew the revolver he had hidden in his trousers and in one swift move, placed the gun firmly against the man's temple and made as if he were about to pull the trigger. "Do not think I am afraid to use it. I am perhaps crazier than you. Do not think I am afraid to die."

"Put your gun away, Señor. We blindfold you, only as a precaution. We are on the same side. We did not want you to be able to describe us, if ever asked. I am glad she is in such good hands," he said to his compadre. "I did not know if you could think on your feet, Señor. I am happy to know who I have entrusted her to. Put your gun away. We are on the same side."

Decker put his gun away.

"Do you know who I am, Señor?"

"Does it matter if I know who you are?"

"It matters that we are friends. It matters that we trust each other. Perhaps it is best if I reveal myself to you." The man removed his blindfold so that Decker could see him. He was struck by how handsome the young man was, how vibrant, well-formed, one of those creatures who was truly comfortable in his own skin, with a sensitivity and passion to his dark eyes that Decker could not help but envy.

"Tell her," the young man said softly, "I wait for her in the mountains. Tell her her father is safe. And when you think it is not dangerous, tell her you will bring her to me. Do you know who I am now, Señor? I am the one who waits for her."

Carlos Castell. "Yes, I know who you are, Carlos. And, now, I will forget that I have seen you."

Would he be able to forget that he had seen him?

He felt like an actor in a stage play who had been hurried backstage for a costume change. He was given a pair of Habanero-style baggy trousers, a white cotton shirt, and a black overcoat that seemed a size too large, and directed to put them on. The effect was to make him look larger, stockier than he was, and when his shoes had been traded in, as well, for a pair of black planter's boots that laced partway up his calf and a small black sombrero had been placed upon his head, he truly resembled a Havana native.

The atmosphere in the apartment was hurried, efficient, as if they understood the urgency of their actions and the precision the next few hours would require.

Decker had concealed beneath his pants, as well as the revolver, a large wrench and his leg had started to bruise as the metal banged relentlessly against him as he walked. Carlos, noticing the rough and red beginnings of the bruise, took the wrench from him, wrapped it in a red bandanna and gave it back to him to conceal again beneath the new trousers.

The three small vials of sulphuric acid, closed with glass stoppers and sealed with wax, were gingerly moved from the pocket of the old shirt to the new. Decker did not want to think about what would happen if they leaked. Carlos concealed them with a handkerchief, jauntily folded as if it were part of his outfit.

"Have you ever done this before?"

"Once, in practice. It took much longer than it ought to have."

"I hope you have enough here to melt the bars," said Carlos. "We have hidden a saw in the cornice of the roof in case you need it." And then Carlos held his arm. "If I do not see you again," he said, "take care of her for me."

Carlos opened the door of the apartment, cautiously, and stood there for a moment as if assessing all was clear. His voice got softer. "Tell her," he said, "I will wait for her in the mountains. Tell her her father is with me and that he is safe. Bring her to me when, if, you feel you are out of danger."

At this moment, Decker wanted to turn and look at his rival, study his face, see if he could see what she saw in him, but he had already seen it. His ally and his rival, one and the same. But when he turned back to say, "Thank you," Carlos had disappeared back into the apartment and shut the door.

Decker did as he was instructed, followed the shorter of the Cuban men down the stairs and onto the street.

"I will take you as far as the beach," said the man who on reflection appeared to be not more than eighteen. "After that, you will be on your own. Walk by the ocean's edge, double back to the alley behind the jail and from there, make your way to O'Farrill Street. They'll be waiting for you. I have been told to wish you luck."

His boots felt heavy on the sand. He walked awkwardly, clumsily, in the fashion of a worker. There was a wind blowing and the palm trees which edged the beach listed to the side, the palm fronds hanging, wan and limp, as if they were in mourning. The air was hot but the night was gray, dark clouds in the sky as if there was about to be a tropical storm. The ocean was gray and choppy. If they were lucky, they would be on a boat in three days' time heading for New York Harbor. There was something comforting about the way the waves broke gently on the shore.

When he reached the dock, he doubled back, to the alley that edged the *Casa de Recojidas*. As he had been directed, he walked through the alley as it zigzagged behind the prison, leading to O'Farrill Street. He was tired but none of them had wanted him to risk a carriage ride and a driver who could say, "Yes, I dropped him at . . . after 10:00." The wind was blowing stronger and the moon was starting to be visible through the clouds. They would not have the protection of a foggy night but conversely, he would be able to see the cross *if* she hung it in the window.

It was almost ten-thirty as he walked quickly through the alley behind the prison, as softly as he could so that you could barely hear his footsteps. There was an eerie quiet, the guards evident on the parapets, almost in silhouette, as if they were frozen there, framed by the still, dark night. He walked, past the prison, two blocks down before he doubled back to the little house on O'Farrill Street.

The front door was open and the poker game was still in play, a half-empty bottle of cognac on the table which he hoped was merely a prop. So far, so good. He took his place at the table, received a pile of matches, and proceeded to win three hands.

"Yes," he said again, as Pedro dealt another hand, "fairly certain I wasn't followed."

There were the sounds of a late night, drunken supper from the house next door, laughter and men shouting over one another. Someone was playing a guitar. The front door to that house was open and when some of the guests began to leave and it seemed as if the neighbors were about to retire, they closed the card game up, blew the candles out, and lay down on the stone floor for an hour to try to get some rest. Only Pedro, who was blessed with the ability to sleep anywhere, was able to rest. Decker lay on the floor, absolutely still, unable to relax, his muscles taut, as if all his senses were on alert.

A few minutes after eleven, "lock-down" at the prison, the bells tolled from the courtyard signifying bedtime. They heard them, strangely melodic for prison bells, in the little house on O'Farrill Street. Lying on the cold stone floor of the front room, Karl Decker thought about Evangelina Cossio y Cisneros. She would be in her cell with her other cellmates. It would be at least an hour before she could make a move. He knew, because they had timed it, that it took almost forty minutes for the guards to douse every third torch in the hallways and throw the prison into semi-darkness.

$\mathcal{T}$he bells which had just tolled from the court-yard echoed through the halls of the *Casa de Recojidas,* as if the sound had chimed and resonated against the individual bars. The other inmates were all in their cells, presumably locked down for the evening.

"Someone told me that ship's comin' and that you're gonna be on it," said Nadine in a whisper that barely carried across the cell. She picked up the chocolate Evangelina had left for her on her cot. "Is that what we're celebratin' here?" she asked. "Is that what this is, your goin' away party."

"The American man gave me chocolates," said

Evangelina. "I try not to think about the transport ship to Ceuta."

"But you've heard the rumours, too, haven't you?"

"I've heard—that a transport ship to Ceuta is due to arrive. Yes. But, I pray that the rumours are not true."

"And if they are?"

"My father taught me," said Evangelina, "that if you live one day at a time and take things just in the order they are given to you, without trying to get ahead of yourself, then all things are possible. It has always worked for him. Today is Monday and Thursday is a long way away. I have heard, yes, that the transport ship to Ceuta is due to arrive but . . ." And then she added very softly, "If you do not see me in the morning and you do not hear shots fired from the square, then you'll know that I am safe. Eat your chocolate, Nadine." She looked at her pointedly. "Perhaps it will help you sleep."

"I would give up a night of sleep, if it would help you."

"And, if you were caught, you would be on the ship to Ceuta with me, too. Eat your chocolate, Nadine. This is not your cause."

"Freedom? Freedom is the cause of every man, woman, and child in Cuba."

But Evangelina shook her head.

Nadine just looked at her and nodded and made a noise in her throat that sounded a bit like, "Hmmmph . . ." She looked at the chocolate for a moment before popping the whole of it into her mouth. "I hope the American man isn't plannin' on givin' me a headache."

Evangelina smiled at her, gratefully.

Anna just sat on the edge of the bed humming. A few weeks before, a guard had unlocked the door to their cell in the middle of the night and led Anna in. She wasn't humming then. She was scared, into silence and submission. She stood there with big eyes just beyond the door where the guard had left her. When he closed the cell door and locked it behind him, Anna just stood there. Evangelina had walked over to her and taken her hand. "It's okay, Anna. It's okay. No one's going to hurt you here." She led her over to the cot and gently urged her to sit down and Anna just sat there on the edge of the cot, humming, the way that she was humming, now. Evangelina walked over to her. And took the small piece of chocolate from the cot where she had left it for her. She held it in her hand and, as if Anna were a child, brought her hand up to her mouth and bade her to eat it. "That's good, Anna. That's good. Slowly, Anna."

Nadine just nodded again and asked if there were anything more she could do for her.

"Pray that the night is kind to me. And that you do not see me in your dreams."

The clouds had dispersed, swept away by the wind which was only now starting to die down. The moon was almost full, a bright sphere in the sky that looked as if it had been hung there, the *Casa de Recojidas* framed, as if it were a fortress, against the night sky, looming large, impenetrable, daunting. And though Decker knew he should not doubt himself, it occurred to him to question the competence of his compadres.

On the face of it, they were a ragtag crew, Hernandon, Miguel, and Pedro, but Decker clung to the notion that they each harbored secret abilities that would become evident before the night was through. Pedro swung the huge ladder clumsily against the wall of the little house, the weight of it being almost more than he could manage. Miguel held it steady, although its legs were not quite even so that it wobbled a bit and stretched the length of the wall at a slight angle.

The prison was shielded by a guard wall which towered twenty-feet-high above their heads. They had been advised it was further protected on the top by a thick sprinkling of glass from broken bottles, a crude but effective deterrent. If they were not cut by it, the noise of their footsteps would most certainly give them away.

Halfway up the ladder now and Decker could just make out the window. But there was no sign of Evangelina. Three-quarters up the ladder and Pedro began to climb up behind him. Pedro handed him a pair of oversized canvas gloves. Decker put them on, his dexterity slightly hampered by their size and awkwardness, as he began to sweep the bits of glass that lined the wall, slowly and carefully, into a large canvas sack that Pedro held open for him. As each tiny shard fell, its sound seemed magnified as the pieces of glass fell upon themselves into the bag. Pedro carefully passed the bag down to Miguel who rested it gently on the ground.

Pedro began to climb the ladder again and Decker looked down to the street as Don José Arroyo, the warden of the prison, walked out of the front gate of the *Casa de Recojidas* and stood on the dirt walkway in front of the jail. Decker was the only one who had the vantage point to see him. He tapped twice on the ladder, the signal for them all to freeze, but Pedro continued his climb up the ladder. Decker tapped twice again and this time his warning was heeded. The three men stopped, absolutely still, but the ladder with Pedro frozen there in mid-ascent was a beacon for disaster. And then, inexplicably, as if he'd simply wanted to get some air, Don José Arroyo walked back into the prison again. It was a moment before any of them relaxed enough to take a breath.

She would always remember the way the cold stone floor felt against the soles of her feet, harsh, rough, her senses in tune with every step she took. She had made the decision not to put her shoes on, she was enough of a country girl to do this barefoot, her version of travelling light.

She would always remember how many steps it had been to the end of the hall, forty-seven, and how she had stayed as close to the wall as she could as if it would somehow hide her. The door to her cell had been left unlocked, compliments of Ernesto Herrara. He would be on guard, on duty, for the next two hours so, if they could only move quickly enough . . . but so far there were no signs that anyone had come to rescue her.

She turned down a corridor that dead-ended. Cut into the wall was a small window, just at chin level, with four metal bars sealing her in. She took the diamond cross from her pocket, undid the clasp and fastened it to one of the bars. She could see the moon in the sky and stars, but still saw no sign of her rescuers. She had never felt more alone in her entire life. She sat down on the cold stone floor to wait.

$\mathcal{K}$arl Decker hoisted himself up on the wall and knelt there, absolutely still, until he was certain no one of the guards on the parapet had noticed him. He could see the window clearly, now, and there was still no sign of Evangelina.

In an instant, Pedro hoisted himself onto the wall. They pulled the ladder up behind them and, in one movement, swung it across to the roof of the prison, as if it were a bridge. It seemed as if an enchanted spell had fallen over the city, the roof of the *Casa de Recojidas* bathed in moonlight. And ever so faintly, as its many facets shimmered slightly, reflected by the light of the moon—Decker saw the glint of the small diamond cross she had hung from the bars.

In a second, Pedro, being the lighter of the two, had crossed and was standing on the roof of the jail. Decker quickly followed. Pedro held his hands as Decker eased himself down to the ledge of the window and, as if she were a vision, something he had seen before only in his dreams, Evangelina stood framed in the darkness of the window.

She reached through the bars and took his hand and they looked at each other, for the first time with no one else observing them.

"We have no time, Evangelina. Stand away from the window."

The window had only four bars that were fairly widely spaced. He fastened on the bar farthest to the left and began to pour the acid, meticulously, drop-by-drop to the bottom of the bar. He could see that it was beginning to do its work, but the process was slow and painstaking, and accompanying it, a faint, noxious smell, almost like rust, the smell of burning metal. He worried that the smell, alone, would give them away.

Evangelina watched from the other side of the window, occasionally shifting her weight from one foot to the other, as if it took all of her strength to keep still.

You have waited much longer than this, Evangelina. He instructed Pedro to find the saw that had been hidden for them. And, when the bar was almost melted through, he resorted to the saw. Damn, it was taking too long to do this. The noise of the saw was terrible but brief as it gave way almost immediately. He said a prayer that nobody had heard them. He pulled the Stilson wrench from his trousers and fastened it to the bar and pulled with all his might until he felt the bar snap. He put the wrench away and put the canvas gloves back on and ripped the bar from the window. One more, only one more bar, and the hole would be large enough for her to climb through. They heard someone stirring in one of the cells. Evangelina made as if she would go back then. "No, stay as you are. No one is coming. We have no time."

He went through the process again, pouring the acid, meticulously drop-by-drop, this time the process was faster but seemed just as slow, painfully slow, and again resorted to the saw, the wrench, put the gloves back on and ripped the second bar from the window. He had barely passed the second bar back to Pedro, when Evangelina made as if she were about to climb out of the window. He pushed her back.

He wiped the sill of the window, carefully, with a cloth to insure that no acid remained. He went to give her his hand but she declined and began to wiggle out of the window on her own as agilely as if she were a mountain cat. When her head and body were halfway out the window, he put his arms around her waist and lifted her onto the thin ledge where he stood. He held her to him for a moment, he felt her breath on his shoulder, her rapid heart beat against his chest.

He went to help her across the ledge but she shook him off. "No," she said, she laughed at him, "I feel as if I could almost fly from here to the other side."

It was remarkable how swiftly she passed onto the roof and across the rungs of the ladder, upright, with only her arms out to keep her balance, as if she was an acrobat who had been trained to this, never losing her footing, despite her bare feet, as though it were the most solid ground she had ever tread on.

Decker followed her, not quite as gracefully or un-eventfully, pausing in the middle on all fours to grip the ladder as it began to wobble and sway uncertainly beneath his weight. It took all of Hernandon's strength to hold it steady or was it Hernandon who had let the ladder slip to begin with and Decker was in danger, for a moment, of toppling the ladder and falling with it to a certain death. It was Evangelina who threw herself down on the ladder to steady it. The two of them exchanged a look as Pedro followed easily. In a moment, the ladder was quickly pulled back across the roof and slid to the ground.

Inside the little house on O'Farrill Street, after they had slipped in the back door and shut it behind them and the house was in darkness and outside the streets seemed still and silent, he felt her take his hand again.

He whispered to her, "If all goes well, I will meet you again in three days. Your father's in the mountains with Carlos. It has been arranged that I will take you there. And then . . . and then, we will talk about what happens then.

"You will go, now, with Hernandon. I wish I could take you myself. But we have been advised not to be seen together within the city's limits. There is a carriage waiting to take you somewhere safe." He did not remember to tell her to trust no one.

$\mathcal{S}$he felt as if her feet barely touched the ground as she struggled to keep up with Hernandon. He was stocky, with big shoulders and dark eyes that seemed to look past her, stolid, yet he moved surprisingly quickly for someone of his size. His footsteps were almost silent, as if he were an Indian guide. He knew the city well and led her to an alley that zigzagged, almost at right angles. In the middle of the alley, he led her through a passage between two houses to a courtyard and out its wooden gate, until they had come, almost in a circle, to the sidewalk of Egido Street where the arranged carriage was to wait for her on the corner. She saw the shape of it underneath an unlit lamppost. She felt as if she were about to take the final steps to freedom.

It was an old carriage, inconspicuous at the curb, two bay horses harnessed to it but when they approached and realized it was driverless, Hernandon put his hand on her arm and stood with her, for a moment, on the sidewalk. He looked around frantically, pretending the vain hope that the driver had grown restless and wandered into a doorway to wait for them. But, of course, there was no sign of him. Appearing to think on his feet, almost as if it were an impulse, Hernandon ushered her into the back of the carriage. He jumped into the front cab and took the reins, grabbed the leather crop on the seat beside him, and struck the horses with it sharply.

In the little house on O'Farrill Street, they heard the clatter of horses' hooves, a staccato rhythmic pounding as the carriage drove away.

*E*vangelina felt as if her heart were beating as quickly as the horses' hooves which were flying across the cobblestones, leaving the *Casa de Recojidas* a distant speck behind them. Hernandon drove the carriage along the waterfront. She could see the moon resting high above the ocean. It had been so long since she had seen the sea, the deep-blue water, dark as the night sky, tipped with white foam as the waves crashed and pounded into the sea wall. It had been so long since she had heard the sea. She had no idea where he was taking her. The complexion of the neighborhood began to change, as if they were driving "uptown," leaving the industrial district behind them. He directed the horses to turn onto a street the name of which she didn't know, where the facades of the houses and buildings were tidier, more elegant, than those in the neighborhood around O'Farrill Street. And because it was the middle of the night and residents were mostly respectable, upright citizens, the streets were deserted, the houses shuttered and dark, as everyone in the neighborhood was sensibly asleep.

He pulled the horses to a stop in front of an imposing stone building with huge French windows on the second floor, each edged by a round balcony like the boxes at the opera. She could see a man standing in the shadow of the front door of the building, in a heavy overcoat, as if he were waiting for them. She dared not think there would be a bed inside with linen sheets to lie on and that someone might have made her a cup of tea. She was aware, underneath the excitement, of how tired she was. She was about to spring from the carriage, even though he had not directed her to, when Hernandon opened the carriage door and she found herself staring down the barrel of a gun.

Evangelina just looked at him. She knew enough not to react. Physically, she was no match for him, and, if she were to scream, in all likelihood, whoever came to rescue her would discover her identity and she would be returned to the *Casa de Recojidas*. It was something her father had taught her. "In battle," he said, "you have a second to react and only a half-a-second to decide not to react." She just sat there, absolutely still, watching Hernandon.

"I am going to put the gun away, Evangelina," Hernandon said, "and you are going to walk before me into the courtyard as if I am escorting you home. Make no mistake, the gun will be beneath my coat, at all times, aimed directly at you, and my instructions are to use it if I need to. They do not care what happens to you, only that you do not fall into the hands of the Americans, that you are not a victory for Mr. Hearst."

She nodded to let him know she'd understood. She began to get out of the carriage, and as she did, heard the sound of horses' hooves behind them on the cobblestones. When she saw Hernandon turn to see who was approaching, she stopped mid-step. He pushed her forcibly back into the carriage. The man who had been hiding in the shadows disappeared into the courtyard.

The events of the next few minutes went so quickly that she had no time to react. Two horses and then two people jumped from them, almost without coming to a stop. She saw a man grab Hernandon from behind. And then, it seemed to be a woman who trained a gun on him. Hernandon fired at her, two shots quickly. The woman had no time to fire back. The second shot had been unnecessary, the first had hit its mark. And the woman fell to the ground as the man who was holding Hernandon from behind pulled a knife and slit Hernandon's throat from left to right.

Evangelina put her hand over her mouth to stifle her scream as the man, who she would later find out was Eduardo Cortez, let Hernandon's limp and bloodied body fall to the ground.

As the word, "Gracias," slipped from Evangelina's mouth, Eduardo Cortez grabbed her by the shoulders and said, "Trust no one."

He bade her get back in the carriage and in one swift motion lifted himself into the driver's box . . . He picked up the crop and was about to strike the horses with it . . .

"What about the girl?" asked Evangelina.

Eduardo Cortez shook his head. "Her name was Ana Maria Varona," he said, "and she would be foolish enough to feel, if she could feel anything anymore, that her sacrifice was worth it. Leave her there. Perhaps we will get lucky and they will mistake her for you."

He struck the horses sharply with the crop and continued to strike them until Evangelina was forced to grip the sides of the seat to keep her balance as the carriage raced across the cobblestones. When he was twenty blocks away, he turned down a street that was lined with single-family houses each with its own courtyard and gates. Even the alley was tidy, as if the servants were forced to sweep there.

He brought the horses to a halt in the middle of the alley, where a small wooden gate entwined with jasmine led to the back of a house. At the top of the gate was a small plaque which said: "No. 22" and beneath it, *"Entrada de los Sirvientes."*

"The man who lives here is a doctor. He is giving, presently, a small soiree. It has run very late. It is intentional that it has done so, intentional that there are many people in the house and none of them have seen you. I will take you to the kitchen where they will hide you and when the last of the guests leave, someone will show you upstairs where a room is waiting for you. Remember what I said. Trust no one."

There was something about the way she looked at him that made him feel he should go on.

"Do you think that the Americans are your friends?" he asked her. "They are not. They have their own interests. Sometimes their interests are the same as 'ours'. You look at me surprised, as if you are surprised to hear me be possessive about your revolution. What did you think? What side did you think I was on?

"They will ask you to go to Washington to see President McKinley—they believe that if you were to testify before him, he would finally authorize, could convince Congress to authorize, the sending of American troops.

"I know what you are capable of. We have been watching you for some time. There is a reason why we chose you. But you will, truly, be on your own, now.

"Yes, I know the risk we run asking for assistance from the Americans, that they could claim Cuba for their own, as they wish to do with Hawaii and Puerto Rico. But, we are a curious, independent people, not so easy to annex. And, without their help, we may never win this war. Do we ask too much of you? It is a choice you have to make.

"You look at me so strangely. No, I will not try to talk you into this. You are right, Evangelina. I am on no one's side. At the moment, you are the most valuable thing I have."

$\mathcal{A}$s he walked her through the gate into the garden, she remembered something her father had said to her, "Until such time as we are free, Evangelina, everything we do will have a price." She had never before thought of herself as a commodity.

As they walked underneath the arbor in the garden, the fragrant smell of the night-blooming jasmine ripe in the air, she realized it was the first time the air had smelled fresh to her since sometime before Batabanó when they'd waited for the ship to take them to the Isle of Pines. That was when the air had turned, when they'd ridden in the train car piled in like cattle, the air thick, musty, gamey, as if it were possible to smell fear in the air, and later that night, were made to sleep on the dock in Batabanó with the sponges that had been left out to dry. She had never before thought of smell as a tangible, pervasive thing one had to live with. As long as she lived, she would never be able to forget the smell of the *Casa de Recojidas*.

There was a rope tied to a willow tree in the garden as if a child had used it for a swing and the night jasmine blooming fresh in the air. As she followed Eduardo Cortez to the door of the house where they would hide her, it occurred to her to wonder how much the smell of jasmine cost.

"Remember what I said. Trust no one. We found the driver, dead in a doorway. That's how we knew to come for you. We may not be in as close proximity to you next time. Trust no one." He left her at the kitchen door, handed her over, so to speak, to a tiny woman who was the cook there, who bade her hide in the pantry until all the guests had left.

When the house seemed quiet, another servant, a mulatto girl, who appeared to be younger even than Evangelina, led her up the back stairs to where a room was waiting. The bed had been turned down. There was an arrangement of flowers in a vase on the bureau, burnt orange lilies mixed with long-stemmed white roses and a few sprigs of a delicate fern. Someone had set out supper for her, a plate of rice and chicken, which she could barely eat. There was a long white nightgown laid out on the bed and fresh towels by a basin of soapy water which smelled a little bit like lilacs. The sheets were linen. The coverlet was satin. There was a Bible on her bedside table. But what she was most struck by was the unobstructed view from the window. It had been three years since she had not been behind bars.

$\mathcal{K}$arl Decker lay on the hard stone floor of the little house until it was almost 4 A.M. There would be only another hour of darkness to protect their flight. He and Miguel slipped out the back door. Pedro would remain in the house until morning at which point he would leave by the front door, as if he were going to work, with the intention to never return.

As Decker was leaving, Pedro smiled at him and said, "Until next time, Señor."

Decker nodded and followed Miguel out through the garden to the alley and, two doors down, through the passage in-between the houses, to the street behind O'Farrill Street. As they turned the corner, he thought he heard something moving in the shadows. Miguel was laughing, loudly recounting a story he'd made up about a drunken girl who'd made a pass at him, in an effort to appear as if they were just coming home from a long night at a bar.

Decker was certain he heard footsteps behind them.

He listened carefully, watching his own feet and Miguel's to time their movements. Yes, there were definitely footsteps behind them. He turned but there was no one there. He put his hand on Miguel's arm, who paid no attention to him. Miguel continued to rant as if he were in a semi-drunken, ebullient state. And Decker sensed, a split-second before it occurred, that he was about to be cornered. There was something strange about the way he could not get Miguel to respond to him.

The footsteps were closer now and faster, gaining on them. He had no doubt they were being followed. He was not surprised when, in the middle of the block, Miguel pushed him into the alley and pulled a machete from his belt. He remembered Eduardo's words, "Trust no one," as Miguel slammed him against the wall and the man who'd been tailing him since he arrived, his "shadow," turned the corner into the alley.

The man pulled a gun and looked as if he was about to use it. Decker put his arms up over his head, in a gesture of surrender, and hoped there would be an opportunity for diplomacy. Miguel turned around and saw the officer in the Guardia Civil (if, in fact, that was who he was), the "shadow," holding the gun on them and dropped his machete instantly to the ground. The man directed Miguel to kneel, head-down, as if he were praying. He handcuffed his wrists tightly behind his back. And then, using his jacket as a silencer, put the pistol against the side of Miguel's head and pulled the trigger. Diplomacy was looking doubtful.

Decker was surprised when the man put the gun away and said, succinctly, in English, without a hint of an accent, "You can thank me later."

*H*is name was Jack. The Cubans called him Joaquín. He preferred the last name of Thomas but had been known in the past to use others. In Havana, he was known as Joaquín Tomás. He was an American by birth and by citizenship, who was presently an officer in the Guardia Civil, a soldier-for-hire, if you will, having recently completed a tour of duty in Santiago, Chile, but he had always kept his ties to the Americans.

When he assigned himself to keep a vigilant watch on "Charles Duval," the reporter from New York who William Randolph Hearst had sent to interview Evangelina Cisneros, no one in Havana questioned his judgment or suspected that he had received a directive from

Hearst himself that it would be "well worth-his-while" if he would keep an eye on Decker. So, from the moment Karl Decker set foot on Cuban soil, Joaquín Tomás had been tailing him, just in case he got into any trouble.

He had been impressed by Decker, how powerful he was and reserved, at the same time, restrained, not the least bit rash, yet able to act quickly, decisively under extraordinary pressure. How, one moment, he could appear notable and slightly flamboyant, and the next, seem innocuous and nondescript. He was well-suited to his chosen occupation. Both of his chosen occupations. He had none of the impetuous, daredevil arrogance that was so common in young, Ivy League men who'd chosen to be war correspondents.

"Tell me," asked Decker when they were safely hidden in the back of a milk truck heading out of the city, "did I ever successfully evade you?"

"We are both quite good at what we do."

$\mathcal{E}$vangelina spent the next three days alone except for the servants who spoke in hushed whispers and brought her tea, or salad, or fresh cakes, depending on the time of day. A few hours before dawn, the fourth morning she was there, there was a discreet knocking at the door. And an old woman's voice said, "Decente?"

Evangelina slipped on a robe and opened the bedroom door. It was the tiny woman who was the cook, and from her manner, Evangelina assumed she had worked there for many years. She was carrying a tray with coffee and fresh bread and a gray dress folded across her arm. She slipped into the room and shut the door behind her.

The woman's voice was raspy, almost like a man's. It had a slight nasal quality made more guttural by the tobacco that she regularly chewed. "The doctor has asked me to tell you," the old cook said, "that his nurse is ill. He wonders if you might work for him today." She had a nurse's uniform thrown over her arm. "He has risked his life for you, you know. We have all risked our lives. Please tell me that it was worth it."

But without waiting for an answer, she laid the uniform on the unmade bed and left the room.

The uniform was just a way to walk her through the streets disguised. The doctor had given his driver the day off and took the reins himself. He said very little to her, except that he hoped that the servants had made her comfortable and that she'd been able to get some rest. Privately, he wondered how the last few years had not left more visible marks on her, no signs of pleurisy or malnutrition. All the scars she had were inside. They stopped at the house of a woman whose child he had delivered a few days before. Evangelina held the baby as he examined him. She marveled at how tiny the child was, how perfectly formed, how it knew so little of life that it looked up at her with nothing but trust in its eyes.

They left the woman's house and got back into the carriage. The doctor said nothing more. He directed the horses west to the outskirts of Havana, then, and seemed to leave the city and take a country road. He stopped in the small town of Mariano at a small roadside cafe and farmacia. He led the horses to the water trough and tied them up and let them drink. He disappeared inside. And then she felt him take his seat again and heard the crack of the whip on the backs of the horses. It was only when they were a mile away and he reached back and took her hand that she realized it was Mr. Duval who was now driving the carriage.

He pulled the carriage to a stop and got into the backseat next to her.

Evangelina was crying, finally, tears from her eyes. He took both her hands in his. "Did you think you would never see me again?"

She remembered Eduardo's words, "Trust no one."

And then he took her in his arms as if he were going to comfort her and, for just one moment, she forgot everything else in the world.

They abandoned the carriage in the stable of a deserted farmhouse (whereabouts of the previous occupants unknown). It had been hastily abandoned, as plates from the last supper were visible on the table through the window, as if the tenants had fled (or been evicted) in the middle of a meal. As had been arranged, two fresh horses waited for them in the paddock.

They rode on horseback, across a field and up a trail that led into the mountains. As they rode deeper into the mountains, the road grew steep and rocky, seemingly less travelled, as Decker had to occasionally dismount and cut the brush away with a machete so that they could continue on. There was a light rain falling. They stopped in a grove of beech trees to let the horses rest. The white trunks streaked with black where they had been soaked by the rain.

"My father would say that the rain signifies a new beginning, Mr. Duval."

"My name is not Mr. Duval. It is Karl Decker. Please, don't be frightened. It's the only thing I've lied to you about. I am a journalist. That part is true but since I have been to Cuba before and spent a lot of time with Gomez and Villela and their men, if I had entered under my given name, they might have suspected me. I'm sure they have deduced it by now." He said his name again, "Karl Decker."

She answered simply, "I will have to get used to that."

He smiled at her.

"Are you taking me to see my father?"

"Yes. And Carlos." Should he tell her, now, his true intention? No, he would save that part for later. And, out of respect, it was a conversation that he should have with her father.

"Are we almost out of danger?"

"No, not yet." Sometimes, her innocence surprised him.

"What do you want from me, Mr. Decker? Surely you did not come all this way and risk your life to unite me with my family."

He would have to tell her, now. "I want—Mr. Hearst wants you to come back with me to New York."

She did not tell him about her conversation with

Eduardo Cortez. "Yes," she said, "I should have suspected that. A young girl wronged. An innocent rescued. It has always been good copy. A pawn in his political game. Is that what I'm to be, then?" She shook her head. "My work is here."

"It is your choice," he said softly, in the hope that he would calm her down, but she would not be silenced.

"A trophy for your Mr. Hearst? Is that what I'm to be then?"

"No. If you like. If you want to call it that. I think he would say, a symbol of the struggle of your country."

"I do not have an answer for you, Sir."

Washington, D.C.

$\mathscr{K}$atherine Decker knew when she walked in the front door that there was someone in the house. Why hadn't she run? Why hadn't she turned and walked out the door, shutting it behind her? Nathan would be still at school, a number of hours yet before he came home. She had sent Marguerite out on errands. There was nobody there to protect. Why hadn't she simply tiptoed out the door and walked away from danger? What proprietary, what possessory instinct compelled her to come in? Because, if she hadn't, she would not have been the woman Karl had married. It was her house and no one had the right to be there unless she had invited them.

She didn't exactly march up the stairs but almost . . . without stopping to take her coat off . . . That's not true, she started, on the fifth stair, to take her coat off, intending to throw it on the straight-backed velvet chair in her bedroom, but as she approached, she realized the smell of cigar smoke was quite strong from her room and, when she opened the door, there was a curious Spanish-looking fellow sitting in the intended straight-backed chair. He wasn't alone, two other slightly dangerous-looking Spanish gentlemen were making themselves quite at home on the window seat. It occurred to her they might be unpredictable since they'd had the poor manners to show up unannounced . . . but she could also exhibit actions that were difficult to call. They had not reckoned on the fact that she would be more intrigued by them than she was frightened.

"I wasn't expecting company, sir," she said to the one who was smoking the cigar on the window-seat. (Someone less sophisticated might have assumed that she ought to have been addressing the one in the straight-backed chair but she knew, the moment she walked in the room, that he was "muscle" and it was the one on the window-seat, curiously the youngest of the three, his shirt unbuttoned in the European style, leaning back against the windows, who seemed to her to be in charge.)

The one in the straight-backed chair stood up as soon as she entered and shut the door to the bedroom behind her, kicked it with his foot. That made her nervous.

She had a bunch of peonies in her hand that she'd brought home from the florist, the green paper they were wrapped in damp and in danger of dripping on the carpet. She set them in a vase on the coffee table.

The one on the window-seat nodded at her respectfully. "We have been expecting you, ma'am."

She couldn't figure out where she could sit. She didn't want to sit on the edge of the bed which rested conspicuously in the center of the room. "I will, with your permission, put some water in these to keep them fresh," she said. She did not want them to know that she was frightened.

"Alfonso, put some water in the vase for the Señora."

She nodded back at him, respectfully, and took her coat off and walked across the room to the closet to hang it up.

Karl had left a shotgun on the shelf just above where her dresses hung, behind the white angora shawl. In one movement, she could have had it in her hands, but he had always cautioned her against this course. "The problem," he said, "with aiming a gun is someone is liable to aim one back." She was certain all three of these men were armed. She hung the coat up and before she could turn around, she felt a man's arm around her neck, clenched at the elbow in a chokehold pressing her against his chest. And she heard the man from the window-seat say, "Do you know where your husband is?"

The one that was holding her spun around with her so she could face her inquisitor.

"He—he left me a note—" It was difficult to speak with the man holding her so tightly. She put her hand on his arm to try to get him to loosen his hold but with his other hand he grabbed hers and pushed it away. She would be no competition for him. "A note that said that he was going to New York. That was five weeks ago. I have not—" her voice wavered uncertainly, "heard from him."

"I need a better answer."

The man who was holding her pulled her back by her hair and though she tried to stifle it, a small cry escaped from her lips. "I do not know where my husband is." The man who was holding her again pulled her back by her hair. Again, she cried out.

"That's enough, Alfonso." The man who was holding her let go her hair but did not release his arm from her neck.

The one on the window-seat spoke again. "Do you know where your son is?" He did not wait for her to answer him. "We know where he is. He's at St. Matthew's, where he should be in the middle of the day. Your husband is in Havana. He is involved in something that he has no business with." His legs were crossed and he looked at her closely as if he were studying her. He took another drag of his cigar. He stood and walked over to her, then past her to the closet. "I never understand why people attempt to make things that do not concern them their business," he said.

He began to examine the clothes on Karl's side of the

closet. "Do you have all your husband's shirts made, Mrs. Decker? There are some here he's never even worn. Oh, I'm afraid I've burned a hole in the sleeve. I'm so sorry." He took it, still on its hanger, and threw it to the floor. "Are you resourceful, Mrs. Decker? Can you get a message to your husband? Tell him, tell him, if he persists, we will make his business ours. Can you remember that, Mrs. Decker? Can you? I'm sure you can.

"Make a little bit of a mess, boys, so Señora Decker does not forget that we were here."

The one who was holding her pulled her hair once more for good measure, then tied her hands behind her back and then her feet and left her on the floor of the closet. They shut her inside. She could hear them as they started to ravage through her bedroom. She could only imagine the objects they were breaking. The Tiffany lamp on her side of the bed that Karl's aunt, Louise Thatcher, had given them as a wedding gift. The vase on the table, it had been her mother's vase, in which she had set the peonies. She was quite certain that was the sound of the Colonial mirror that hung, that used to hang, over the mantel of the fireplace smashing to the floor. Its glass was gray and mottled and she had never liked the way she looked in it, anyway.

$\mathcal{A}$re we almost safe?"

It reminded Decker of Nathan, in a way, as if Evangelina were a child saying, every hour or so, "Are we almost there? . . . Are we there, yet?" Or in this case, "Are we safe?"

Conventional wisdom was the Spanish would not dare to follow them into the mountains, nor would the Guardia Civil. The mountains belonged to the rebels. But there was nothing conventional about this and he did not know to what extraordinary means General Weyler would go to recover them.

"One would hope that we were almost safe. What are you expecting, Evangelina?"

She didn't know if that were a personal question or a political one. "I want to go home," she said, "what I really want, is to go home."

If he did not know her better, he would think that she was close to tears.

"I realize," she said, "that I, sometimes, still think I have a house somewhere, that my sisters are in the kitchen and it smells of coffee and cornmeal and cinnamon, and my father is out in the field. That the Beauchamps are in the big house expecting visitors for tea. That everything outside remained the same. That this has all been a dream, an illusion, that I will someday magically wake up from."

If I could only make that so, Evangelina. Out loud he said, "You have a choice to make, Evangelina. I do not envy you that choice. You can stay with your father and Carlos in the mountains and fight, as you always said you would, by their side . . ."

She nodded.

"You can join your sisters in the small fishing village where they are hiding. You can—"

She finished the sentence for him. "Decide that we are working for something more important than my personal happiness."

Good girl. It was her spirit he was falling in love with.

"I do not know if I have the strength—not to make a decision. But to do what you ask me to do. You think

I am stronger than I am. You think the last three years have not extracted a price from me, that they ought to have made me more resolute. I am tired, Mr. Decker."

"Karl."

"Karl." It was the first time she had said his name.

Washington, D.C.

The little doorway on 18th Street was dark, the morning paper still on the steps, as though no one had been there yet that day. Set into the door, a brass placard, engraved with the words:

GITLIN'S BOOKS & CURIOS

and directly underneath it:

BY APPOINTMENT ONLY

Katherine Decker looked in the window of the store to see if there was evidence of anyone inside. The interior of the bookshop was tidier than one would have thought for the volume of material it contained, as if every one of the books had been dusted, catalogued, and precisely placed, with the spine out at the edge of the shelf, so that each was easily accessible. In the back of the shop was a glass display case in which were literary and historical documents, a personal note from President McKinley on White House stationery, an original signed draft of the Declaration of Independence, an Elizabeth Barrett Browning sonnet, on parchment, in her own hand. Ancient maps of sea voyages were framed and hung on the walls and the shop always smelled faintly of tea and pipe tobacco. She hesitated in the doorway.

She had gone with Marguerite to St. Matthew's to pick up Nathan from school. It had taken a bit to calm Marguerite down, brandy, on each of their parts, and a strength she did not know that she possessed. Marguerite had quickly cleaned the debris in the bedroom (yes, she had been right about the Colonial mirror) while Katherine had changed her dress, slipped into a simple suit and boots and taken a long coat from the closet and a pair of gloves. She had directed Marguerite to pack a small suitcase for Nathan.

Sometimes he looked so much like Karl, like a younger miniature version, with his perfect posture and those pale eyes that seemed to have an understanding far beyond his years, and a sweet and calming sensitivity. He'd put his hand on Katherine's arm as they were riding in the carriage to Tess's house and said, "Don't worry, Mama. Whatever's troubling you. Remember what Grandpa used to say, 'Today's problems are tomorrow's accomplishments.' "

She had dropped them at her sister Tess's house and left a fairly cryptic note:

> Dear Tessa,
>   Please take care of Nathan and Marguerite for me. They are to stay with you. I'll try to be back by supper and will explain all then.
>
>   Love,
>   Kit

That was what her sister had always called her when she was little, "Kit," and she had called her Tessa. There was something reassuring about writing their childhood names.

She had hailed a carriage outside her sister's house and taken it to *The Journal*'s D.C. office, but when she had seen two of her assailants lurking on the sidewalk, she directed the driver to continue on to 18th Street to Gitlin's bookshop. Karl had always told her if she ever had an urgent problem and she could not get to New York to see Mr. Hawthorne, that she should go to Gitlin's Books. It was just one of the many odd things he had told her and urged her to remember.

The small electric lamp was on, on the desk in the back of Gitlin's shop, and a big striped cat was curled up, lazily, in the corner. She suspected the cat lived there whether anyone were in the shop or not. She rang the bell. It was a few moments before she saw Mr. Gitlin appear from the back room. He had on a gray pinstriped suit that seemed quite threadbare and was a little short at the ankles, wire spectacles framed his eyes. Katherine would have guessed that he was close to sixty although his sandy hair was only just flecked with white. She and Karl imagined that he had piles of money stuffed under his mattress and hidden in secret compartments in the bookshelf walls. He peered at her through the window in the door. He seemed not to recognize her. (That was not the case, he knew who she was instantly, but in the event that she had simply come to buy a book, he would request that she come back tomorrow.)

"We are not open for business today." He had a slight German accent even though he had lived in the United States for most of his adult life. "If you will pass your card under the door, I will try to make an appointment for you."

Katherine took one of her calling cards from her purse. She wrote on the back of it. She passed it under the door.

He looked at the card. *Mrs. Karl Decker*. She'd written on the back of the card, *Request an appointment,* now. She had underlined the last word twice. Gitlin unlocked the door. The moment she was inside, he locked it again and pulled the blinds down on the windows.

"You've been expecting me."

"I knew it was a possibility."

$\mathcal{G}$itlin took her into the back room he used as a study. She sat on a tattered couch, her hands folded on her lap, trying not to behave like a child and pick at the white bolts of stuffing that peeked out suggestively where the upholstery was torn. It did not take much for him to get the whole of her story.

There was something sobering about his crisp Germanic delivery. "Would you recognize these men if you saw them again."

"Yes," her voice quavered, "I have seen them again. They were outside *The Journal*'s offices, two of them, anyway, which is why I came here. I thought, if I went to *The Journal*'s offices, I might be able to get a message to Karl. And then I remembered, Karl had always told me, if I had a problem, I was to come here. Do you know where my husband is, Mr. Gitlin?"

"Not exactly. You did not go to the authorities, might I ask why?"

"My first thought was for Nathan. And my second— Karl had always told me that if I were in trouble I was to come here." She asked again, "Do you know where my husband is, Mr. Gitlin?"

"I know where he is meant to be."

He disappeared into the front of the shop and came back, a few moments later, with a yellowed, rolled-up parchment which he laid out on the desk. It was drawn in black ink and affixed with the royal seal of the Spanish Monarchy.

"Do you know what this is, Mrs. Decker?"

"A map, of a sea voyage, detailing a route around Cuba and Jamaica, if I'm not mistaken."

"It's a map, of Columbus' second voyage, on the *Niña*, when he travelled to Cuba, erroneously thinking it a limb to China, and under the impression he would find gold and temples and cosmopolitan cities. He returned home, almost in disgrace, but it was on that journey when he set the Spanish sovereign flag and a large wooden cross into the beach at Cape Maisí and claimed Cuba for Spain.

"Your husband is in Havana or in the mountains just outside Havana. And if Columbus had not travelled to Cuba in 1493, mistakenly thinking it the Chinese province of Mangi, then none of this would have happened.

"Do I know where your husband is? Not precisely." He got up and walked across the room. He took a sheaf of letters from an envelope on a shelf. "I think you should read these."

The first was on parchment, ornately decorated in its border with an American flag, an eagle, a lion, a Spanish flag, and at the bottom, two hands shaking, and atop the hands, on either side, E Pluribus . . . Unum. In elaborate calligraphy, the letter read:

To Her Majesty

Maria Cristina

In the name of civilization . . . and humanity, we, the undersigned . . . American citizens, ask Your Majesty to extend your royal protection to Evangelina Cossio Cisneros, now lying in prison in Havana and threatened with a sentence of twenty years' imprisonment. . . .

We ask you to set this innocent young girl free and send her to live among the women of the United States. . . .

"I have seen this—I have read this petition, Mr. Gitlin. I was one of the twenty thousand women who signed it . . . What does this have to do with my husband?"

"Have you followed her story since?"

174

"A bit. I think so."

"Then you know that it did not have the desired effect. That Miss Cisneros was sentenced to be remanded to the penal colony in Africa, Ceuta, where no one has ever survived. She has the distinction of being the first woman to be sentenced there. Your husband has gone— your husband went to Cuba to rescue Evangelina Cisneros."

Her reaction was the same as Karl's. *Rescue. Had they gone mad?* And then immediately *The Journal*'s slogan flashed before her eyes. *While others talk, "The Journal" acts.*

"Correct me, Mrs. Decker, but you would not love him if he had done otherwise. He would not be the man you had married, if he had not agreed."

"Wouldn't I, Mr. Gitlin? I am politically curious. I know more than you think. I know that Cuba is valuable to us, not just for its agriculture, but its strategic placement, as well. And I am quite conflicted about whether we have the right to intercede. I am not naïve. I know that we have tried to buy Cuba from the Spanish twice before. And, I am not convinced that a 'free' Cuba is our aim. And, yet, at the same time I am female. Do you know how many nights I've sat up wondering where Karl is? This isn't the first time he's gone off. And, does my mind go to lofty things? It does not. Sometimes, I imagine him with other women . . . And, in this case, I would be partly right. No, he would not be the man I had married if he had not agreed. But, people change,

Mr. Gitlin. Life has a way of changing them. And, now that he has put my son at risk. Now that you have put my son at risk . . ."

"We will take measures to protect you."

"And is it within your power to protect him? To what lengths will Mr. Hearst go to sell his newspapers? Or does he have interests that extend beyond his publishing?"

"He has successfully broken Miss Cisneros out of prison . . . They have not yet"—Mr. Gitlin's voice was clipped, well measured—"left the island of Cuba."

"They . . . ?"

"It is our hope that he brings Evangelina Cisneros back with him to New York. When you read about it in the paper, about her successful break from prison, you will know that they are safely at sea, on a ship heading toward the United States."

"And that Mr. Hearst," she added, "has boosted his circulation one more time, and that we are closer to an act of war. If you will excuse me, Mr. Gitlin. I am late for supper with my son."

"Wait, Katherine." He called her by her first name. "You are not behaving like the woman that I know."

She turned back to face him. "Am I not, Mr. Gitlin? People change."

He could see that Evangelina was, as she had said, very tired, not as strong as she appeared. He worried that she would not make the ride. They needed to find a place to rest. Fresh horses. A meal.

He worried that they could not ride through the night without attracting unwanted, unnecessary attention. Their presence in the day was plausible. But at night they would appear conspicuous if they were discovered, out of place, on horseback, without even a carriage to protect her. Why had they not sought shelter? They would appear as if they were fleeing from something, to be what they were, escapees, hunted. The American and the Cuban girl. His Spanish was not quite good enough, his

skin too pale . . . they would not pass if they were discovered. Riding in the night like refugees.

The distance from Havana to Cienfuegos was 210 kilometres (approximately 130 miles). He had been told that
they would be waiting for them in the mountains about
thirty kilometres shy of Cienfuegos in a canyon called
El Cañón de los Fantasmas. A canyon that was not on
the map. Evangelina told him of the local legend, that
it was a canyon inhabited by spirits, that the mountains
had a way of holding on to sound, but she was vague
about its exact location. Thirty kilometres outside Cienfuegos? Forty? Difficult to tell from the description he'd
been given. And, he did not know how far they had yet
to go. Travelling straight through was far too dangerous
with only the stars to guide them.

So far, they had not made good time, stopping to rest
each hour or so, lingering so that Evangelina could smell
the eucalyptus and the pine and the calabash trees and
so that she could take her shoes off and feel the earth
beneath her feet. By mid-afternoon, she was so weak,
he had to help her back onto her horse. As he lifted her,
she reminded him of a fragile bird. He felt her heart
beat. No, she was not as strong as she appeared. And
he, too, felt tired.

They had made no contingency plan for stopping
overnight. There would be no hotel or inn by the side
of the road waiting to receive them. Nor could they

reasonably throw themselves on the mercy of strangers or risk hiding in the brush. They needed a place to find shelter. They needed a place to hide, under the protection of someone powerful enough to shield them, respectable enough to be above suspicion. And then he remembered the Hanovers. Sanderson Hanover III. Betsy and Sandy Hanover's plantation. Betsy would give them refuge. She would hide them for as long as necessary. Going to Betsy, was like going home.

In between the small towns of Madruga and San José de las Lajas, down a dirt road edged with fields of sugar cane, the air damp and saccharine with its smell, a gatepost, at the top of which was a wooden sign that read RANCHO DE LA DULCE NADA. In Spanish it meant nothing, Ranch of Sweet Nothing, but in English, Ranch of Sweet Nothings. And he knew it was Betsy's joke, Betsy's play on words. In fact, it was what she'd said to Karl about Sandy when she'd first met him, that she could happily do nothing with him for hours, that they had a natural comfort with each other, in addition to everything else. He wondered if he had ever had that with Katherine, that sort of ease where they could spend hours with each other, unoccupied hours, when the door was closed, alone, content to simply be in each other's presence. His life with Katherine was so much about form, so carefully constructed and maintained. Katherine was so terribly independent, which was probably why she could suffer his absences. He always imagined that she was strong enough to bear whatever came her way, that she would, in fact, be quite all right alone. He could not see the Hanovers being content to be without each other's company for any length of time. That they would always need to be within some proximity of sweet nothings.

Evangelina looked slightly wary of the long driveway to the house. The sun had set and there were shadows all around them. There was barely a thumbnail's crescent of a moon and only a few stars visible in the sky. There were cane fields all around them. It reminded her of the Beauchamps'. She tried not to remember the morning when the Spanish had come and taken her father away.

They left their horses tied to the trunk of an ash tree and went the rest of the way by foot. There was a moment when it seemed too far to go back and it seemed as if the road before them would never end. And then they saw the faint outline of the house at the end of the roadway. There were lights visible burning inside the windows. As they approached, the old collie began to bark. He took Evangelina's hand.

They walked, steadily, noiselessly, almost as if they were moving in synchronicity. Decker put his hand out, fist closed, as the collie neared him, and it quietened and began to walk the rest of the way with them, like a sentry leading them around the side of the house past the small herb garden Betsy Hanover had planted to the back kitchen door.

No one in Cuba locked or bolted their doors (except the Spanish) but all were armed with some sort of weapon, knives, guns, and even small children were schooled in their use. Decker knew none of the servants who worked for the Hanovers. He approached with some caution. He bade Evangelina wait by the side of the house and, without knocking, carefully turned the handle of the back door, and pushed the door softly open.

Betsy was alone in the kitchen. She did not hear him as he entered and walked softly across the room toward her. He put his hand on her back. She turned and looked up at him and kissed him on his cheek. She hugged him for a moment. She seemed not to want to let him go. "We've been so terribly worried," she told him. "The entire country's on alert. The army has been mobilized. You've put them to a lot of trouble. There were rumours they had captured you."

"Not so easy to hold me down," he said. "You should know that by now."

She managed a smile. "We have rooms waiting for you," she said. "I thought that you might come here. Is she with you?"

He nodded.

"There were rumours she had been killed."

"We had hoped for that—it was one of the women who helped us. No, she's just outside."

"Oh, and were you planning to leave her there? Where are your manners?"

It was only a moment before Evangelina was taken from the side of the house and brought into the warmth and comfort of the kitchen. A kettle put up to boil. A plate of chicken fetched from the pantry, fresh bread, a bowl of fruit, and many different kinds of cheese. As Betsy was just in the process of preparing a plate of food, she saw Evangelina grip the counter of the kitchen as if to hold herself up. Karl was by her side immediately, his arms around her, helping her to stand.

"I'm all right," she said quite softly, her voice a little breathy. "I just felt a little weak. I'm quite all right, now."

The way Karl looked at her, rushed to her side, the way he put his arms around her waist to steady her, the way she answered, soft, almost a whisper in his ear, none of it was lost on Betsy Hanover.

"How could you be all right?" she said, her voice betraying none of her suspicions, except that it was oddly clipped. "I would not be if I had gone through half of what you have. Sandy," she directed her husband who had just walked into the kitchen, "carry her into the living room. I'll be in, in just a moment with a tray."

Sandy Hanover did as his wife had bid him, picked

Evangelina up in his arms. He was surprised at how light she was, not more than 90 pounds he guessed, and the trusting way that she put her arms around his neck as he lifted her given they only had met, actually not been formally introduced, a few moments before. He carried her sitting, across his arms, the way you would carry a child or a bride over a threshold, into the living room and laid her on a couch. He took the wool afghan, sensibly plaid, that Betsy always left folded on the arm of the sofa and laid it over her. He walked across the room to the heavy cabinet against the wall, opened it, and took out the cut-glass decanter and a crystal glass. He poured a shot of brandy.

"Here, drink this, child," he said. "It will give you strength. And damn what your father would say to you."

"On the contrary, Mr. Hanover"—she took the glass from him—"I drink to my father which I'm sure he would appreciate at this juncture. And to all he stands for. And all he has taught me to believe. And to you and Mrs. Hanover for having the grace to give us shelter." And she downed the brandy in one sip.

Sandy Hanover, understandably, had the same reaction to her that all men did, although his eye and his affections would never stray from Betsy, that she was extraordinarily poised for one so young, and that there was something so appealing about her spirit and her physical form, that he was quite awed, impressed by her.

"I would feel better if you joined me."

He poured himself a shot of brandy and sat in the chair beside her. "You are safe here, you know," he said. "We will see that no harm can come to you or Karl."

And, for the first time in years, Evangelina felt as though that might be true.

In the kitchen, as Betsy carefully and quickly carved the chicken and the bread and laid it on a plate, she studied him, her childhood friend. "Are you quite certain," she asked him, "that you know what you have taken on?"

"I have always been ambitious, Betsy."

"I ask you one thing and you answer quite another. We can play this game if you like. I will bring her food to her and you will sit here in the kitchen and think about how you will answer me."

"Am I to be scolded, Betsy?"

"No, questioned."

Sometimes one's friends are more aware of our actions than we are ourselves. Sometimes they recognize our behavior before we recognize it ourselves.

"Are you sure," she said, when she returned, "you know what you have taken on? Are you sure you know what you're involved in? Have you measured all you risk? I will say no more. It's not my place to speak to you. You have always been—and I hope we can remain so—quite dear to me . . ."—she repeated it—"as if we are distant cousins of a sort. But I cannot witness what I have just seen and not say something . . ."

"What would you say to me?"

"I would say that you have a wife and child at home who wait for you . . . and I will say no more."

Washington, D.C.

What is the nature of an obsession, what delineates the fine line that separates it from a true and functional love? Or could such a distinction be made if the person in question is the one that you are married to?

It was as if every waking, every sleeping moment (yes, even in her dreams), Katherine held on to thoughts of him. There was no interim space, no breath, between when she awoke and the moment when he entered her thoughts.

She had never been like this before. She had always been practical, self-reliant, efficient, optimistic. No, you could not say that she was happy all the time, but reliably cheerful. But she felt, now, as if she were a part of something she had no control of and the dark spectre of it loomed over her, enveloped her, uncontrollably, almost as if it were a force of nature. Yes, everyone had noticed, she had changed.

She said very little. Her sister, Tess, could not quite make sense of what *had* occurred. Marguerite's account was fractured and guarded. And Katherine said nothing instructive, at all, except that it all had to do with some story Karl was working on and until he returned to the country, it made more sense for them to stay with her. If that was all right, of course.

Nathan was the only one who seemed to understand it, intuitively. He had his father's innate calm and almost fatalistic understanding. He took it on himself to soothe his mother in a way that was both grown-up and child-like, at the same time. He would come into her bedroom in the middle of the night and say, "Mommy, can I sleep with you?" feigning he was too afraid to be alone but, in fact, his intention was to comfort her. And it was effective, if for no other reason than that she would not allow herself to break down in front of her son.

She tried to hold on to something Karl had said to her when they were first married. "If we are ever separated," he said, "remember that we are in this together." She wondered what she would do if he never returned.

$\mathcal{T}$hey had left the Hanover Plantation a little before five. Betsy had packed a lunch, sausages, chicken, cheese, a flask of wine, as if they were going on a picnic after a morning's foxhunt, but they would be quite grateful for its provisions as the day wore on. It was not yet light and a mist hung over the mountains. They rode quickly and as the sun rose, the earth turned from pink to gold, bathed in an almost other-worldly glow as they made their way upward into the mountains.

Horses' hooves pounding. Staccato, insistent, as if someone were gaining ground on them. Difficult to tell how many, as the sound reverberated through the mountains, falling back upon itself in staccato repetition.

El Cañón de los Fantasmas. These were not the sounds of phantom horses chasing them . . .

"Tell me . . . are you frightened?"

"No," she answered. "I am past the point of fear."

"They would not follow us this far into the mountains. I am certain of it."

"Would they not, Mr. Decker?" She laughed. "I am an embarrassment to them. And you are a humiliation. And my father, if they were lucky enough to capture him, would be a trophy. We are a symbol of all they fight against, a tangible prize to hold as an example. *If you defy us, then . . .* " She gestured with her hand. "In answer to your question, Mr. Deck—" She corrected herself, "Karl, they cannot break my spirit." Her voice was challenging. "How quickly can you ride?"

She did not wait for him to answer her. In a moment she was off, as if she were traversing the softest pasture, her mount secure, as if she were one with the horse who fairly flew across and upward on the rocky mountain trail as if it were a filly though he knew for certain it was almost nine years old. And in true competitive spirit, he kept up with her, almost as if they were taunting each other to see which one could go the faster.

But as quickly as they rode, deeper into the mountains, higher as the trail twisted and turned and narrowed, their pursuers seemed to gain on them. And their numbers seemed to increase.

"It is an illusion," she insisted. "There are not as many horses as you're hearing. The sound has a way of echoing and there are those who believe that on some days you can hear the hoofbeats of horses that passed here years before."

"When you feel the ground shake beneath you, Evangelina, it is no illusion. We could send the horses on ahead and hope that they would act as decoys . . . But I do not know what would happen to us then."

Evangelina answered for him. "We would take our chances in the Canyon of the Ghosts. And hope that we did not become part of its legend. I know the way. It's not much farther. If we could hide from them, when it was dark, I could lead you there."

When he reached up to lift her from the horse and his arms circled around her waist and he lifted her toward him and for just one moment, they were aware of each other's breathing. A moment frozen in time in the middle of a day that otherwise moved too quickly. As he lifted her to the ground, they were aware not just of each other's breathing but of each other's hearts beating, as well. And then he slapped the back of his horse and sent it galloping off into the mountains. Evangelina's followed, leaving a cloud of dust, spinning, like a small typhoon in its wake. Their eyes locked, for a moment, before he took her hand and pulled her with him into the brush at the side of the road.

"If you move quickly through, it will not scratch you," she told him but it was too late, a branch had already made its mark across his cheek. "Just here," she said, "a bed of moss. We should not go too far from the road."

How long they lay there, motionless, like small animals trying to blend into the landscape? Long enough for the sun to move westward in the sky and drop below the mountains and the sounds of night, a coyote howling, the mournful call of an owl on its own, the wind rustling through the trees, to invent a landscape of their own. Evangelina wanted to wait until it was completely dark before they made their way back to the road. Too long. As Karl Decker's heart beat faster, in keeping with his breath, as he heard the sound of horses' hooves grow closer and, then, closer still and, then, stop on the road exactly in front of the place where they were hiding. He was surprised at how calmly Evangelina sat there, how in control she was of her own stillness, how implacable her expression, determined yet soft, passive yet defiant, as if she could face and possibly beat back, by sheer strength of will, whatever came her way.

The bushes parted. Roughly. With barely so much as a warning. As he reached up to protect her, he heard someone speak her name: "Evangelina." It was Carlos, and there was a way he pronounced her name, with the "g" soft, that made Karl realize, he himself could never speak her name that way.

In a moment, she was in Carlos' arms, unmindful that anyone was watching them.

They made him feel at home, as at home as they could, in the makeshift village that was their campsite. They heralded him as a hero but he sensed that many of them were wary of, as they saw him, "this man from New York who had been sent by Mr. Hearst to rescue her," all except for Evangelina's father, who was effusive yet almost sage-like in his demeanor. He had a white shock of hair and dark piercing eyes that seemed to belong to a much younger man, strangely out of place, strangely incongruous except for the vast amounts of wisdom that they seemed to hold. His name was Augustin Cossio but no one ever called him by name, they simply called him "Señor." After dinner, he sat Decker by the campfire, as if he were instructing him.

"It makes no difference," he said, "if the Spanish recall Weyler. You know that, don't you? They will just replace him with someone else, another general, who will appear for the first month to be slightly more humanitarian than Valeriano and will turn out to be equally as ruthless." He smiled. "Do I sound jaded? I am an old man, Mr. Decker. For much of my life, my country has been in the state you see it in now. This is the second incarnation of the revolutionary government, the government in arms, as we call it. See how grand our offices are. See how proudly we wear our uniforms."

From this last remark, Decker understood where Evangelina got her humour, the sad collection of torn trousers and shirts worn by the men around him could hardly be called uniforms. He went on, "We are proud. But without the help of your country . . ."

Carlos interrupted him. "Without the help of *his* country we might stand on our own, Señor."

"As we are standing now?" the old man asked softly, with just a bit of an edge.

But Carlos would not be silenced. "José Martí felt," he said, "that the United States . . ." There was a way he said United States, enunciating each syllable, that made it sound menacing. "The possibility," he went on, "of a Cuban annexation by the United States was the greatest threat of all to the independence of our island."

"And where is José Martí, now?" the old man countered.

Carlos looked angry. Evangelina lost in thought. Decker made the decision not to intercede.

"You want me to go with him to New York, don't you, Papa?"

"Do I have the right," her father asked her, "to influence your decision? No. It is yours alone. I have"—this last was said softly—"influenced so much of your life. You did not choose to be a soldier's daughter."

"No, Papa, but I would choose—" she said it again with stronger emphasis, "I *would* choose to be your daughter."

*W*ith what sadness did she make that last journey, dressed as a boy, in a blue serge suit with a necktie at her collar and a big slouch hat pulled over her head underneath which her hair had been slicked down with pomade and cut, in the front, so that she resembled the young sailor boy she was impersonating, as she smoked a large cigar which made her lightheaded and giddy.

Outwardly, she appeared calm, resolute, possessed of an inner strength that was admirable and surprising. In front of her father, as the rest of the men had gathered to watch them say good-bye, she had not betrayed any emotion, feeling as if the mantle of their struggle had truly passed to her—she was no longer just a soldier's daughter . . . but a soldier, now, herself. A soldier does not admit that he questions the principles he stands on or the actions he must take. Not outwardly. But if anyone had looked too closely, they would have seen the sorrow in her eyes which was, luckily, in keeping with a young boy going off to sea.

The night before, after everyone had gone to bed, she had had occasion to speak to her Papa for the longest time. He was sentimental, she could not ever remember him being sentimental before. He was always stoic, matter-of-fact about what lay before him. But now it was as if he were lost in thought and memory. He told her about the first time he met her mother. "She was no older than you are now. And I was only two years more than you are. I thought I had never seen anything more beautiful. You look like her, you know. She had the most perfect skin, flawless, and deep, dark eyes that seemed to dance whenever anyone said the slightest thing amusing. It was her gift, the way she could look at you, as if you were the most interesting person she'd ever seen. I have been blessed to have had a perfect love." He made Evangelina lay her head in his lap as if she were a little girl.

"I know she would be proud of you, Evangelina. I do not know if she would approve of the way that I have raised you."

She sat up and looked at him. "Papa, no apologies, no regrets, remember . . . that's what we always promised."

But, it was as if he wanted her forgiveness for what she had been made to go through. "We had such dreams, Evangelina."

"We still have dreams. We, none of us, chose this, Papa. Say it after me, Papa. No regrets."

"No regrets."

And by way of further reassurance, although it would seem he ought to be the one who was reassuring her, all she could say was, "I would not be who I am if it were not for you. I would not choose to be anyone else's. I am a soldier's daughter."

They talked about her sisters. She tried to convince her Papa to go and live with them.

"No, they are too headstrong, these young men of yours. Too impulsive. And though they only listen to me some of the time, those few times are worth it. Go to him. He did not choose this either."

She kissed her Papa. She waited until he'd made his bed on the straw mat beneath the beech trees and wrapped himself in a woolen blanket, securely, underneath the stars.

Carlos waited for her by the campfire, and she lay with him until it had burned down and was just an orange glow of embers and the sun began to rise in the sky.

*C*arlos had made the decision that Karl Decker and Evangelina Cisneros would travel separately to Havana. The authorities were looking for an American and a Cuban girl. Best not to let them find what they were looking for.

Decker had left the night before, immediately after sundown, on horseback, in the company of two young men, dressed as if they were cowboys. They had spent the night in the cowhands' bunk at a cattle ranch owned by a rich but sympathetic Cuban. General Weyler maintained that all the ranchers were sympathetic out of fear, but for some, it was a love of country.

Evangelina left the camp just after sunrise and rode in a modest carriage to Havana. Carlos was driving the horses. He was almost sullen. Not that he ever said much but this was deliberate. The intimacy of the night before forgotten. In the cold, hard light of day, he was just a revolutionary, brash and, as her father would say, head-strong. He knew that it was not for him to approve or disapprove of her decision. As he admitted, it had been hers, alone, to make, but personally and politically, he disagreed with it. They were both of them silent for much of the journey, under the shadow of a dark, un-spoken premonition that they might never see one an-other again. She reached up at one point and took his hand.

How many good-byes did she say that morning? To each flower, each branch, each tree, each blade of grass, and passing sparrow. With what new eyes did she ob-serve so closely the landscape she had taken for granted for so many years. To her sisters who she would have no opportunity to see and whose spirit she would carry in her heart. To her father, her dearest papa. To Carlos, although she would try her best to imagine that she was by his side.

When they were almost to the city, he pulled the horses to a stop and got into the cab beside her. He waited for her to speak.

"Should I tell you," she asked him, "that I wish it had been different?"

He did not answer her, so she went on. "Should I tell you that I wish I had not made this choice, that I wish I had never had this choice to make?"

She grabbed his hand because he did not seem to be listening to her. "Would I sound like a spoiled child if I said, I wish we had a house somewhere and there were children playing in the yard. And my sisters were there with me in the kitchen. Why is this not to be for us? My papa and I have always promised, no apologies, no regrets, but why were we born into a time when our personal happiness must be put aside for some greater good. Or do we just imagine we are more important than we are?"

And, in that moment, Carlos became, once again, just the young man she had met in Cienfuegos, before the events of their country had pushed their lives away. He took her in his arms, the hat she was wearing pushed off her head, his lips found hers, because in that moment it was all he had to offer her, their embrace made more fervent by the knowledge that it might well be their last.

"Should I tell you," he asked her softly, "that I wish I had a house by the ocean to offer you, a castle built out of stone into the cliffs, with windows that looked out onto the sea, that I wish we had days before us with nothing to do but listen to the waves as they break steadily against the rocks, certain that each one will be followed by another. That I wish I had a future to offer you," and then the realization of what lay before them intruded and he continued, "not a dark and inchoate mass of uncertainty. That more than anything, I wish I could give you a refuge, a home of any kind. I wish I could say that I am not jealous of what he has to offer you, the protection of his Western capitalist society, the protection of his Mr. Hearst."

"You cannot mean that. We are all of us on the same side."

"Yes . . . and still I am frightened of what you will become when they make you their talisman."

Evangelina laughed. "I do not know," she said, "that I have ever been a good luck piece for anyone, Carlos. I am a good fighter, but I do not know that I have ever brought anyone luck."

"For me, you have. And I fear what will happen to me if I lose you." He took her in his arms. "You have always been the thing that I am fighting for." He pulled her to him and felt her pull away, almost imperceptibly, as if in that moment, she had already left him.

There was no time, no chance, no opportunity for a final good-bye when they parted. She was handed off like a small child (or a parcel in a relay game), a few blocks away from the wharf. As if it were a practiced maneuver, one moment, she was walking beside Carlos, he continued walking, forward, straight across the busy intersection to the other side of the street, as Eduardo Cortez put his hand lightly on her back and directed her to turn the corner with him.

She turned back and watched Carlos as he walked away from her and barely whispered to herself, "I love you." All the while, she kept puffing on the big cigar in the hope that the smoke would obscure a clear view of her face.

Eduardo Cortez whispered in her ear, "Remember what I said. Trust no one. They will regard you as long as you are valuable to them, but once you have served your purpose, they are liable to forget who you are. I know what I speak about. I have lived this way myself for far too long. You have been a child up until now. You may not think so, but it's true. Decisions have been made for you. Now, you will have only yourself to look to.

"Are you frightened?"

She shook her head.

"Good. Fear is not a good companion.

"But remember what I said, trust no one, and I never thought I would say this to anyone, because I am far too cynical to think this—trust your heart."

The *Seneca* was a small, reliable, seaworthy schooner that had made the trip from Havana to the States and back again many times before. A little bit like old money, its modest but sturdy exterior concealed that within were well-appointed staterooms with rosewood walls and mahogany bedposts and a wine cellar fit for a French hotel. Scheduled to leave for New York that afternoon, it sat anchored, just at sea, a few hundred yards from the wharf in Havana, a fleet of small boats tied to the moorings, waiting to bring its passengers aboard.

The dock was crowded with families saying tearful good-byes, lovers locked in a last embrace, Americans going home and, a little off to the side, General Weyler, standing on the dock in full but informal military dress, his captain's cap pulled down on his head casting a shadow on his already dark features, as he carefully observed the Chief of Police who was checking the passports of the shipboarding passengers, and next to him, Joaquín Tomás who took advantage of his official position to study Decker, without acknowledgement of any kind, or was there a slight nod visible.

Decker resisted the impulse to stop and have a final conversation with him (remembering his training that it is always at the end that one has the tendency to be careless). He kept his head bowed underneath his planter's hat, hunching his shoulders as he carried the wicker suitcases, frayed and bulging and decorated with brightly colored emblems, taking large and heavy steps in his planter's boots, emulating the Cuban peasant he was impersonating. Juan José Aurelio Sanchez y Flores. *Couldn't they have given him a few less names?* And cautioned him to remember the Cuban fashion of naming— Sanchez was his father's last name, Flores, his mother's.

Keeping his eyes down, in the custom of a humble Cuban worker, he took his place in line behind the other boarding passengers. The wharf was chaotic, a large Cuban family in front of him saying a tearful farewell to their 19-year-old son, a Cuban woman with a baby who appeared not to have the proper papers and whose hysterical pleas were not the least bit persuasive or, in any event, were falling on deaf ears. Decker knew she was a "plant", that she had been sent by Eduardo Cortez to divert attention from them and her performance was worthy of the Italian Opera. She was crying now, pulling her hair. "Qué voy hacer? Qué voy hacer?" Which translated as: What do I do? What am I to do? The baby was crying, too, as if caught up in his mother's hysteria. She went on, "Mi esposo espera en Nueva York." My husband waits for me in New York. "Quién cuidara de mi bebé?" Who will take care of my baby? As the baby's wails punctuated her statement. "Qué voy hacer . . . ?" What am I to do? She was crying as they pulled her away from the small boat that was waiting to take passengers aboard the *Seneca*.

The passport that Evangelina carried was for Juan Sola, age 18, sailor by profession. The officer who examined it passed her in a second, he did not even look up to see her face. Decker watched her, from his place in line, relieved when she got into the small rowboat, jammed in between the suitcases and the other passengers, and set her wicker case beneath her and sat on it.

When he reached the front of the line, the Chief of Police held his passport for the longest time. "Have you any money?" the man asked him, finally.

Money? Was he asking him for a bribe. "Sí, Señor," he answered.

"Good," said the officer. "The Americans do not like immigrants," he explained, "who do not have any money." He handed him back his passport and his papers and moved on to the next person in line. Decker felt someone take his arm and looked into the face of Joaquín Tomás. "Have you been to New York before, young man?"

Decker kept his head down, although he could not help it that he glanced up at him. "No, Señor."

"Perhaps you will not like the climate there. In which case, we would welcome your return."

"Gracias, Señor."

Decker took his place in the next line at the edge of the dock and waited for, what seemed to him, an interminably long time, as another small rowboat loaded, which had no space for him, and a second one was buoyed to the dock. He kept his head down. He resisted the impulse to turn back and look at General Weyler. It seemed strange to him that, at the end, there would be no opportunity for discourse.

He noted with some satisfaction that Evangelina was already at sea, halfway to the *Seneca*. No one seemed to pay her any mind. The other passengers had their eyes fastened on the dock, waving to their loved ones as they said good-bye.

When they were halfway to the *Seneca,* Evangelina allowed herself to look back at the shoreline, which was fast receding in the distance, the ocean like glass, the Spanish-built Fort Morro, the castle built of stone, dominating the eastern entrance to the harbor, like a symbol. With what sadness did she say a last good-bye.

When the little rowboat anchored just beside the *Seneca,* she climbed the rope ladder onto the deck and felt someone take her arm. She looked into the face of an old sailor, his skin rough and craggy from years at sea. "Stay behind me," he said.

She followed him to a little cabin on the lower deck. He opened the door and told her to go in. "Lie beneath the lowest berth and do not move, no matter what," he instructed her, "until you are certain that we are safely at sea." He shut the door behind her and left her alone in the cabin. She did not allow herself to think about what would happen if she were discovered.

She hid her suitcase on the small shelf in the closet and then did as he bid her, crawled beneath the lowest berth, the wood planks of the ship's floor, rough and hard beneath her. She lay there, as silent and still as if it were a coffin. She could hear her heart still beating fast but as it calmed, she realized how glad she was to be there.

$\mathcal{H}$ow long she lay under the berth, she did not know. It seemed a lifetime with no way of knowing whether day had turned to night . . . with no way of knowing whether Karl Decker was safe and had, also, reached the *Seneca* undetected.

She felt a slight motion of the boat, but, no, it was just swaying on its moorings. She thought she heard someone coming and knew she had no explanation except the truth, if they were to find her. She thought she felt the boat move again, but, no, it was just rocking on the waves. Her back and shoulders hurt from trying to lie so still. And then she heard the door of the small cabin open and a man's footsteps. The door closed behind him.

"Evangelina." She knew who it was from the way he pronounced her name, sounding the "g," the American way, but she did not trust that he was alone.

"Evangelina . . . ," he called again, "we are quite at sea."

She moved quickly from under the bunk and stood to face him. His arms found their way around her . . . or was it Evangelina who found her way, inexplicably, into his arms. Alone in the stateroom, safely nine miles out to sea, at the end of a very long and dangerous journey with no one there except each other, it did not occur to either of them that they were being disloyal to anyone.

Washington, D.C.
October 23, 1897

$\mathcal{K}$atherine Decker was sitting at the small writing desk in the parlor of her sister's house. The morning sun was coming in the windows, falling in rainbow patterns across the old oak floor. There was a collection of notes and cards in ordered piles spread out in front of her on the desk, invitations to dinner, to tea, that she had not bothered to respond to, calling cards (that had been dropped through the mail slot in the door of the house she shared with Karl) by friends whose visits she had missed. For weeks, she had not responded to anyone.

Her sister, Tess, was quite annoyed, worried, really, but she masked it behind a big-sister bossiness, and offered to go with her to any soirée she felt she could attend. "You need to get out," she said. "You can't shut yourself away here as if you are in mourning."

"In hiding, more like it," said Katherine.

"At the very least, you must respond," her sister, Tess, insisted. "People will begin to talk."

"People, I presume," said Katherine, "are already talking."

And though, at her sister's urging, she had taken her place at the desk that morning with the intention of catching up on her correspondence, so far, she had not written any note, at all. She thought she would start with the more formal invitations, the ones that were easier to decline, an invitation to the Gallery of Art for a John Singer Sargent exhibition (that she would very much have liked to attend but she would not have known how to answer the simplest questions—Where was Karl? When would he be returning?—and she no longer knew how to pretend), a Junior League luncheon (that she hadn't wanted to go to, anyway), etc., and then work her way back to apologies for the occasions and friends she had already missed. That was her plan, anyway.

She wrote a note on her personal stationery to the Women of the Junior League. "I am so sorry," she wrote, "that I will not be able to attend, I have a prior engagement." She signed her name, Mrs. Karl Decker, and slipped it into an envelope. She was still considering the Sargent invitation when she heard the four chimes of the doorbell. It did not, at first, occur to her to get up and answer it. Marguerite would do that or Tess's housekeeper, Selma. But when it rang again, and immediately after, another time, so that the chimes seemed to double up on one another, she realized it was likely she might be alone in the house.

She slid open the big wood doors to the parlor and went into the entrance hall. She was aware of the insistent, hollow sound that her heels made as they clicked across the checkerboard tiles, somehow punctuating her belief that she was alone. She was slightly hesitant about flinging the doorway open to whoever might be on the other side but then she became angry that anyone dared to make her afraid or inhibited, and it was with some sense of abandon that she threw open the front door.

Mr. Gitlin was standing in the doorway. He was wearing an old tweed overcoat and a woolen scarf, a felt hat that was so worn its color was difficult to determine, pulled down on his brow. He was carrying a newspaper under his arm.

"Might I come in, for a moment, Mrs. Decker?" he asked very politely, his accent making the request seem all the more reserved and formal.

She stepped aside and allowed him to walk into the entrance hall. "Please, come into the parlor," she said.

What could he have come to tell her?

"I seem to be quite alone but if you wait for a minute, I will make you tea."

"No, nothing at all," said Mr. Gitlin.

She slid the doors of the parlor closed and waited for him to take a seat on the sofa but he remained standing.

"Have you seen this?" He handed her a copy of the *New York Journal*. Front page story with the headline in bold letters:

FREEDOM AT LAST
FOR THE FLOWER OF CUBA!!

And underneath, the by-line, "Charles Duval."

"That was the name Karl used in Cuba," Gitlin explained. " 'Charles Duval.' As I told you before, when you read this in the paper, it means that they are safely en route to New York Harbor. They are on an ocean liner called the *Seneca* that will dock in four days' time."

"They?"

"Evangelina Cisneros is with him. She is coming to make a plea to the United States for her country."

"That must please your Mr. Hearst. The flower of Cuba will arrive in New York and I am sure he has planned a spectacular welcome."

"He is, of course, pleased that they are safely on their way to New York. We have taken the liberty," he went on, "of making you a train reservation . . ."

"Why would you assume—"

"That you would want to go to New York to greet your husband? I assumed nothing, Katherine. I thought it appropriate that it be your choice and wanted to make any arrangements necessary if those were your wishes." He knew from the last time he'd dealt with her that any decision that was made, she would have to feel was hers.

She looked at the paper she was holding in her hand. The by-line was a fiction but she recognized his writing style. "Despite Weyler's spies, the guards in the street, and a cordon about the city . . ." He had used the name Duval but, in the piece, revealed his true identity, as if he were flaunting his deception for the Spanish.

He had been successful, then. Had she ever doubted that he would be? Yes. She had worried. She had doubted that he would be coming home. And still she feared that he was not coming home to her. "I have, of course, prayed for this, Mr. Gitlin. I will go to New York to meet him. How could I do otherwise? Thank you." At that, she sat on the sofa, as if she were suddenly very tired.

"I cannot pretend that the last few weeks have not been difficult for me," she said. "How could they have been otherwise. I hope that you will forgive my behavior, which must have seemed strange to you."

"Under the circumstances, I do not think your behavior has been strange."

"Thank you, for that, as well."

"No, do not thank me. I imagine that you would not have chosen any of this. But we live in difficult times and sometimes the battles we are involved in are about more than our personal happiness."

"Yes, if I were in my right mind, that is something that I should have said to you."

He gave her the envelope in which were the train ticket and a handwritten itinerary detailing her hotel information and the scheduled arrival of the *Seneca*.

"Will you be coming, Mr. Gitlin?"

"No, you know I don't like to take a front-row seat. But will you come and have tea with me in the back of the shop when it's over and tell me what it was like? They have planned a rally at the dock and a ticker-tape parade the next day in Madison Square and a party that evening at Delmonico's."

"Yes," said Katherine Decker, in a tone that was difficult to read, "as I said, I suspected there would be fanfare." She laughed and her voice got very soft. "Commotion, more like it, just the thing to flame the passions of the nation. I will come and tell you about it, Mr. Gitlin, but you must promise that you will never repeat my telling."

$\mathcal{A}$board the *Seneca*, it was as if they were in an isolated, rarefied space that the world could not intrude on, temporarily cut off from any intelligence from Cuba or the United States. They stayed below in the small cabin, alone, for many hours, with no sense of day or night. There had always been bars between them and a distance created by their circumstances and position. It was as if neither of them realized how close they had become. And when he finally crossed the room and took her in his arms, and she began to kiss him back almost before his lips found hers and felt his hands lightly pass across her body, she realized that she was in love with him.

Afterward, they slept, the way that lovers do, en-twined in each other's arms, aware, even in their sleep, of the one that they were holding.

When they were far enough at sea that there was no longer any danger, Karl Decker asked if she would like to go on deck with him and see what freedom felt like.

There was a part of her that knew—liberty would only truly be when she could stand on the shores of her own country, barefoot, the ocean gentle at her feet, and know that there were no Spanish soldiers on any street corner or makeshift rebel villages in the hills. But she allowed him to take her hand and lead her up the stairs to the deck, well-equipped for leisure, lined with lounge chairs and small tables, blankets available from the stew-ards, if you wanted to sit by the sea.

They walked to the forward deck, their bodies sway-ing slightly as the ship rocked steadily across the ocean. The fresh spray of the ocean, soft across her face which was framed by a mass of dark curls that fell gently around it. He thought he had never seen anything more beautiful. The horizon was clear, as if they were the only ship at sea.

That evening they were the guests of the Captain for dinner. It was then that Evangelina realized everything had changed, that to everyone in America she would be treated as if she were a grand lady.

Betsy Hanover had packed a number of dresses for

her in one of Decker's suitcases, theorizing that if someone discovered them, he could explain that the dresses he packed were "a gift for a lady." He realized, when Betsy said it, that he had not brought Katherine anything, no black lace mantilla or shawl, no Cuban artifact, except Evangelina, and he did not know how Katherine would receive her. He had not brought a gift for Nathan either, no toy or souvenir. (That would be easier to remedy, he would purchase, aboard the ship, a small wooden replica of the *Seneca* and keep each of the hand-painted menus detailing the evening meal, their borders decorated with palm trees and Cuban natives in brightly colored dress, and tie them with a ribbon as a memento.)

That first evening, Decker sent the suitcase down to Evangelina's cabin with a steward, inventing some excuse about how it had been mistakenly delivered to his room. The steward, who was in his 60's and had been a valet for many years, was well-accustomed to the peculiar relations of the upper class. But, still, he thought it slightly odd (having not yet heard the shiptalk that related Evangelina Cisneros' history) that a woman that young and beautiful was travelling unchaperoned. Yet there was something so elegant and refined about the way she conducted herself when she answered the door that he offered to unpack the clothes and hang them for her, as he would have done for any proper lady.

"No," she insisted, "I can quite do that myself." It occurred to Evangelina that it was the first time, in three years, that she had dressed for dinner and just as long since she had had a choice of what to wear.

They kept mostly to themselves. Everyone aboard the *Seneca* knew her story and she was treated a bit like a princess, revered at a distance. Many of the ladies on board assembled a care package for her, a basket of soaps and creams and powder for her cheeks. The simple act of sitting on the deck in the sun and brushing her hair seemed like such a luxury.

It was ten days' journey to New York and as they approached the city, the color of the ocean seemed to change to gray. The size and power of Manhattan were evident to her, at first glance, a city built of stone and glass on an island that seemed rooted to the sea, as if steel casings bound it to the ocean floor. There was no "sway" in its movement. The Statue of Liberty which, too, seemed held securely in its place, with its burning torch, a copper beacon in the distance.

She felt Decker tense when they caught sight of it, as if he knew their time together was somehow over, their hiatus ended. He let go of her hand as they walked down the gangplank. She steadied herself against the rope at the side of the walkway as she realized that the crowd was there for her.

*T*here were almost two thousand people there to greet them. Many of them, the society women who had affixed their names to the numerous petitions drawn up for her, who thought it would be "just the thing" that afternoon, something they could tell their children, that they had welcomed Miss Cisneros at the dock. It was certainly of benefit to tomorrow's paper whose headline would scream: EVANGELINA CISNEROS FINALLY REACHES THE LAND OF LIBERTY! "And the women of America embraced her."

Katherine Decker, standing in the crowd, her face partly hidden by a hat, the veil of which she had discreetly pulled down, was nervous and trying, outwardly, to appear calm.

He was coming home to her. Thank God for that. But some sixth sense warned her that it might not be an easy transition. The crowd was overwhelming to Katherine, she imagined what it must be to Miss Cisneros and thought it strange that she could feel sympathy (and even admiration) for someone who she felt so threatened by.

The veil was not to hide the tears of joy that she was certain she would shed when she saw him walking down the gangplank, but to hide the hurt and jealousy that would be hers when she saw the "Flower of Cuba" walking by his side. "Don't do this today, Katherine. This is what you've prayed for, that he would be coming safely home to you."

But she knew, when she saw him, that it had not been invention on her part. He was, in fact, holding Miss Cisneros' hand at the top of the gangplank and he held it high for all the crowd to see and then, as if some sense of propriety gripped him, he let go her hand, and seeming to falter, gripped the rope railing for support.

$\mathcal{K}$arl didn't look tired. He looked rejuvenated, as if he'd been on vacation or on an adventure, and the expression on his face made Katherine want to scream. He was tan, well-rested, and certainly well-pleased with himself. Did he think that she suspected nothing . . . ? That in the telling of his story, she couldn't read between the lines.

That first evening, Katherine and Karl had dined with Julian Hawthorne and his wife, Elaine, at a small French restaurant on 52nd Street. Evangelina Cisneros had begged off their evening plans, saying she was tired from the journey. But Miss Cisneros was so much the topic of conversation that she might, as well, have been present at the table.

"You would quite like her, Katherine," said Julian Hawthorne who had spent the afternoon with the girl and, not surprisingly, she had had the same effect on him that she had on every other man who met her. "She's quite extraordinary," he insisted.

And probably that was true, under other circumstances, Katherine might have quite liked her, taken her under her wing, made quite a fuss of her. Katherine might have appreciated all aspects of her, under other circumstances, even the side she recognized immediately as manipulative and cunning. Didn't they realize the girl quite knew how to capitalize on her own innocence? "Will you tell them that I am not a young girl wronged?" Didn't they realize she was using them as much as they were using her?

Katherine sat and listened as Karl recounted his story, leaving out, she felt, some personal detail. There was a way he said her name, "Evangelina," softly, almost reverentially, that made her want to throw small bits of china against the closest wall.

But underneath the anger and the jealousy, the rage, if you will, her heart was breaking and it took all of her finishing-school training to smile, as if she felt nothing, at all.

$\mathcal{T}$he next morning, Karl Decker left his hotel very early. Neither he nor Katherine had slept well, as if they were unaccustomed to lying next to one another. As if there were many things unsaid.

His intention was to go to the offices of the *New York Journal*. The air in the city was cold, a wet wind blowing off the park that left him chilled. He thought about going to Evangelina's hotel room. He knew she would not yet be awake. She would answer the door with her hair down, her robe lightly tied. He would put his arms around her waist as he undid the sash of her robe. But he could not leave his wife's bed and go to another's . . .

The night before, he had observed Katherine at

dinner. She probably thought he hadn't, that he had been so caught up in the thrill of his own success that he hadn't noticed her. He'd seen something in her eyes he'd never seen before, sadness, unease. He recalled the first time he had seen her, at a garden party in Virginia. She was only twenty then, with the perfect slim figure of a debutante, her chestnut hair pinned loosely above the nape of her neck, and how he had wondered what she would look like if it fell about her shoulders. He had noted how she chose to dress, in a pale green party frock with barely any frills or bustles, cut simply at the neck, just below her collar-bone, a simple sapphire necklace at the base of her throat, the only visible concession, besides her physical bearing, to her stature. But what attracted him was the way she held her head, the way she laughed, as if none of it was affected and she was perfectly at ease with who she was. He wondered how deeply the last few months had affected her and if he was correct in his assumption that she had never needed him to protect her.

He pulled the collar of his overcoat closed around his neck, as the wind continued to blow across the park. He had a moment where he longed for the warm tropical air of Havana, the slow pace of the cafés, the strains of Caribbean music from a house on the corner, and then he stepped back from the curb as he narrowly missed being hit by a hansom cab in the morning rush of Manhattan.

*T*o Carlos, Havana had seemed the same as always. True, there were soldiers posted on every corner, Spanish and Guardia Civil, with swords at their sides and the bulge of a pistol evident beneath their jackets, but Havana seemed to go on as before, almost to thrive, as if the character of the city could not be altered or subdued or restricted by military rule. The cafes and bars were full, the small family-owned stores enjoying a brisk business, children clinging to their mothers' skirts as they were dragged around for daily shopping, the smell of fresh yeast, sugar, and cornmeal wafted out of the panaderías whose lines of customers edged onto the sidewalk. It made him angry. As if the city were under a spell, a collective unconscious state of bliss and well-being. He heard the distant toll of a ship's bell, long and mournful.

Had Evangelina reached the ship yet? Was she safely onboard and hiding in someone's cabin? Was her heart breaking the way that his was, now?

All he wanted was to leave Havana and go back to the campsite where there were others like him who felt that there was something there worth fighting for. *Viva Cuba Libre*. No one had taught him that it is always at the end that one has the tendency to be careless.

A horse waited, behind the blacksmith's shop, a large black stallion aptly named Midnight, "Media Noche." Packed inside its saddlebags, a knife, a wedge of farmer's cheese, fresh bread, a flask of wine, a flask of water, fresh oranges, and, as if someone had worried about him travelling alone, a leather-bound Bible, in the event he needed to find solace.

He rode quickly, recklessly, away from the city, staying along the waterfront, at first, and as the complexion of the neighborhood began to change, he rode more slowly through "Miramar" (its English meaning: with a view to the sea), the area of expensive and elegant houses in Havana. He was aware of how grand the houses seemed, how cloistered, how out of reach, as if Havana and particularly the residents of Miramar were part of a sprawling metropolis that was out of touch with the struggle of its country.

There was a story circulating among the intelligentsia about Frederic Remington, the American artist who had recently been sent to Havana by William Randolph Hearst to cover the "war." Remington, who had grown quickly bored with the seemingly peaceful Havana, had cabled Mr. Hearst for permission to come home, stating simply:

Everything is quiet. There is no trouble. There will be no war. I wish to come home.

Hearst had cabled back immediately:

Please remain. You furnish the pictures and I'll furnish the war.

Carlos wondered if Evangelina knew what they really had in mind for her . . . He stayed on back residential streets in an effort to keep out of sight and resisted the impulse to ride as quickly as he could away from Havana.

The sun was beginning to set when he reached the foot of the mountains, their pyramid-like shapes framed in the purple glow of the setting sun. Feeling confident, as if he were safe, protected by the mountain roads he knew so well, he quickened his pace and rode on, faster still, unmindful of the horses' hooves that followed him. Echoes of horses that had passed before. El Cañón de los Fantasmas. They shot him from behind, a single bullet lodged directly in his heart. He never even heard the gunshot as his voice became one of the Spirits in the canyon.

$\mathcal{T}$he newsroom of the *New York Journal* smelled, as it always did, musty and intense, a mixture of cigarette smoke, sweat, and ink from tomorrow's paper. There was something comforting about the activity of the newsroom, the chaos and ordered confusion, the constant noise, as if it were at the hub or the center of whatever was going on at any given moment, as its members recounted the news of the day, and the printing press in the basement recorded it, runnning continuously, like a ship's engine, vibrating through the upper halls of the office. Many of his associates rose to greet him, one by one, as if it were a wave across the newsroom. He went directly to Julian Hawthorne's office. There were some things that never changed, the smell of the newsroom and Julian Hawthorne behind his desk smoking his pipe, the dark green blotter as neat as an accountant's.

"You look as though you could use some coffee," said Hawthorne, "we have a long day in front of us."

"That would probably be a good idea."

Hawthorne summoned a copy boy to bring them cups of coffee. The young boy looked at Decker with admiration and respect.

After the young boy left the room, Hawthorne looked at him for a moment. "We have known each other for a long time, Karl."

"Yes, since I was a copy boy."

"And I used to yell at you. I am too old to yell, now. I have to tell you, though, I must confess, this one made me nervous, this last month made me nervous. And though I am pleased with what has happened, Hearst is ecstatic, I'm not sure we didn't overstep our bounds. There are some who believe it is our job to report the news, not necessarily to partake in it. But that's a longer debate and we have no time for that today. If something had happened to you, I would have felt responsible. And, I am afraid, it has become, for you, personal, in a way that nothing else has been."

"Yes, and Pulitzer has accused us of making it up." There was a piece that had run that morning in *The World* that said that Decker had bribed the guards and invented the escape . . ."

"Do you care? We know the truth of it. A bit of controversy is always good."

"Is it?"

"Do we care when it has had a successful outcome . . ."

"Has it?" Decker's voice was flat. "We have yet to see how it ends. We have still to see what will happen if the U.S. does send troops."

"Yet, you are to be commended. You have become as famous as the story you were writing . . . They say we have invented a new kind of journalism. That is not a bad thing. We live in unusual times and you have done what was required. But, I worry," said Julian Hawthorne, "if you are too involved what will happen to you when this story is over?"

"Because I am involved with her?"

"Because you are involved with her? Forgive my bluntness. Because you are in love with her."

"Is it so apparent?"

"Yes. And it has taken some turns none of us expected. We have had a telegraph this morning. Carlos Castell has been killed. He was ambushed by the Spaniards on his way back to camp. Hearst isn't sure that we should tell her, now, at least until today's events are over and she has gone to Washington to see President McKinley. He doesn't know what her reaction will be."

"If I know her, at all," said Karl, "it will only make her more determined."

"I thought that you would want to tell her," said Julian Hawthorne.

"Why would I *want* to tell her that?"

"I thought you might want to write his story, too."

"No, I will leave that to the boys in the newsroom."

There were many curtains on the windows of her hotel room, three layers, gauze for that hour between dusk and sunset—when one wanted still to see the view but did not want to be observed; a layer that was heavy, the palest teal, almost like burlap, to keep out the light in the morning; and, at the top and sides, a layer that was mostly decorative, dark green with pale embroidered flowers, held back by ties made of the same fabric, hooked onto sconces that were a blush of yellow hand-blown glass in the shape of camellias. Evangelina wondered, for a moment, what it would be like if she were to stay in his world. And then was interrupted by a light knock on her hotel room door.

"Something has happened," Evangelina said when she opened the door of her hotel room. "I see it in your face. I have caused a problem for you."

"Yes. But that is not why I have come."

"When a man is—torn," she said, "between two women, we make excuses for him. When a woman engages in similar behavior, we call her a tramp, a hussy, we say her character is not good, that she is cheap and not to be trusted. We are supposed to control our hearts. You have given me so much, and what have I brought you . . ."

"What have I brought you? I wish I was not bringing you this news—"

"You're making me afraid . . ."

"I wish I didn't feel, in some way, responsible. There is no way to soften what I have to tell you. Carlos has been—killed. He was on his way back to the camp, the Spanish Army was waiting for him . . ."

"In the act of saving me . . ." Her voice was clipped.

She realized that when she had left Carlos in Havana, she had not promised him that she would see him again.

She appeared distant, as though her face had been set, cast in the finest porcelain, except her eyes were vacant as if she had been lost somewhere. "Will you understand," she said, her voice barely a whisper, "if I ask you to leave?"

"Of course, I understand. We—you cannot blame yourself for what has happened."

"I wish"—her voice wavered when she said it—"I wish to be alone for awhile."

Did she throw herself down on the bed when he left? No. She walked over to the window and looked out at Fifth Avenue, whose sounds and appearance were so different from the ones in Cienfuegos, at an elegant hansom cab whose interior was upholstered in leather and the woman sitting in the backseat, her hair pinned beneath a stylish hat, her hands tucked securely in a fur muff, and who seemed to have nothing more important on her mind than that she might be late for tea.

And as the carriage passed, the sound of its wheels on cobblestones was replaced, in her mind, by a volley of gunfire, like small taps that rang out angry and insistent in the distance.

Carmen, Costanza, Cecilia. Where are you? Papa. Papa.

And then she was running on the beach in Cienfuegos, the breeze from the ocean blowing softly across her face, as the waves broke gently into shore.

Carlos . . .

She could hear the sound of hoofbeats up ahead. Carlos beside her on Silver.

She would never ride with him on the beach again.

When she looked down onto the street again. It was as if nothing whatsoever had changed. There were children tugging on their mothers' coats. A man rushing by as if he were late for a meeting. A crowd of people waiting at a bus stop. As if oblivious to the fact that, for her, nothing would ever be the same.

*H*er hotel suite had every amenity, a fireplace that was always lit in case one came in with a chill, a rosewood writing desk with a delicate chair, just the right size for a young lady, a sofa by the window to curl up and read on or entertain one's guests. Julian Hawthorne, the editor of the *New York Journal,* had given her a present of a silver quilled pen, his wife had sent over a box of notecards, tied with a satin ribbon, engraved with her name which she had already had many occasions to use. There was a large basket of fruit on the coffee table, in the center of which, among the persimmons, dried figs, pears, and tangerines, was a pineapple, as if someone had gone to enormous trouble to make her feel a bit at home. A vase of white roses on the end-table from Karl with a card that read, in his hand:

Para el amigo sincero que me da su mano franca.

For the honest friend who freely offers me his hand. It was a line from the José Martí poem "Una Rosa Blanca." And she could not help but finish it in her mind.

"Y para el cruel que me arranca . . ."
And for the brute who tears from me . . .
"El corazón con que vivo . . ."
The heart with which I live . . .
"Cardo ni oruga cultivo:
Cultivo la rosa blanca."
I nurture neither grubs nor thistles,
But cultivate white roses.

There was a knock on the door. It occurred to her that she did not have to answer it. She went into the bedroom and sat down at the vanity. She took the pins out of her hair until it fell around her face, long, except where she had cut the fringe around her forehead, there was something about remembering when she had cut her hair, Carlos watching her, teasing as she did it, and how he had taken a lock of it and pressed it between the folds of his wallet, the last day she had seen him . . . The knock again. More insistent, this time. She got up and walked to the door in the living room. She could not possibly see anyone. She was not in shape to see anyone, at all. "Yes, please."

"Evangelina Cisneros," a voice said from the other side of the door. She did not answer him at first, so he went on. "Señorita Cisneros. It is Julian Hawthorne. It's time for us to leave."

She had forgotten, there was to be a ticker-tape parade that afternoon in Madison Square to celebrate her rescue and her safe arrival in New York. What right did she have to celebrate her safety? But this was what she had come to New York for . . . and, if his death were to mean anything, at all, she would ride in the carriage, with her chin up, head slightly down, as if she were proud of the struggle of her country. She would give a speech—a speech for all the men who had been killed, for all the women who had lost sons, and husbands, and lovers. She would give a speech for Carlos. And then, the next day, she would go to Washington and see President McKinley and make a plea for her country and ask him to finally convince Congress to send U.S. troops to Cuba.

"Un momentito, Señor," she answered. "I am not quite ready. I am," her voice wavered, "afraid the time got away from me. Un momentito, Señor. I will try to hurry."

She looked again at the vase of white roses.

And for the brute who tears from me the heart with which I live, I nurture neither grubs nor thistles, but cultivate white roses.

She sat in the front of a carriage, flowers all around her, appearing graceful, elegant, and modest, in a white couturiere gown, her hair pinned up, no jewelry except the small diamond cross around her neck on the delicate chain that Karl had given her to use as a sign in their rescue. Outwardly, she showed no signs of the ordeal that she had been through or the loss that she had suffered. Innocent and pure, the flower of Cuba. Karl Decker sat beside her, wearing one of the white shirts that Katherine had made for him, underneath a formal topcoat, his shoulders back, well-groomed, well-manicured, his face set in a public persona smile, as the crowd regaled him as a hero. And, on his other side,

Katherine Decker, demure and elegant, smiling, as she had been trained to all her life, holding on to her husband's arm.

Thousands had gathered to watch the procession. They rode along the New York City streets from the Waldorf-Astoria, down Park Avenue, to Madison Square, behind an honour guard of soldiers, policemen, and white-uniformed naval cadets, all marching in synchronized step to New York's finest marching band. Julia Ward Howe rode in the carriage before them, and, as homage to her, the band started out with "The Battle Hymn of the Republic."

Mine eyes have seen the glory of the coming of the
Lord . . .

The crowd joined in as they marched along:

He is trampling out the vintage where the grapes of
wrath are stored;
He hath loosed the fateful lightning of His terrible
swift sword;
His truth is marching on.

. . . Glory! Glory! Hallelujah!
Glory! Glory! Hallelujah! . . .

Evangelina felt strangely empowered by it, as if she were part of something much bigger than even she understood. As the crowd led by the marching band segued into an arousing John Philip Sousa march, she looked down at the faces of the American women, many of whom had written letters from their hearts, in an effort to secure her release, wrapped in warm coats, well-fed, well-rested, beneficent, even, with rosy-cheeked children at their side. America seemed so clean to her—scratch below the surface and you would find the exterior and the interior cut from the same wholesome cloth, without the passions and conflicts and strife that threatened to tear her country apart.

As they were showered by handfuls of brightly colored confetti and long, thin ribbons of ticker tape by the throngs of people in the street and the many spectators that crowded the open windows of the buildings on Park Avenue, the irony that they were being showered with the capitalist symbols of yesterday's stock prices and yesterday's news was not lost on Karl Decker.

He looked over at Evangelina. He remembered the white-sand beaches, the soft velvety leaves of the calabash trees, the open expanse of the mountains. He wondered what would happen to the Cuba that he loved, if the Americans were to annex it. He felt Katherine, beside him, take his hand and he was jolted back to the present. He heard the people on the sidewalk screaming his name and Evangelina's as the carriage rode past. Katherine smiled at him. Evangelina just sat there looking regal and demure.

She heard Carlos' voice, "José Martí believed that a

possible annexation by the United States was far more dangerous than . . ." But where was Carlos now? And without the help of the United States, she knew for certain, another young woman in Cuba would lose the man she loved.

A small wooden stage had been erected in Madison Square and the carriage cut a line through the pressing crowd and stopped in front of the steps to the stage. Katherine Decker watched as Evangelina was helped from the carriage by three white-uniformed naval officers. They took her arm with white-gloved hands and escorted her and Mr. Decker to the bandstand. Katherine was left there by herself, without direction—should she go up on the bandstand or stay below in the crowd. For a moment, she felt abandoned and then Julian Hawthorne took her arm and bade her sit next to him in the small bleachers that had been set up just below the stage. She watched as Karl and Evangelina took their places and the crowd went wild.

To Evangelina, it was as if she were in a dream that someone else had manufactured. As if William Randolph Hearst had created an illusion. And she was the illusion. The crowd cheered so loudly that she was momentarily deafened by it, excited and frightened at the same time. And there were shouts of "Evang-e-lina" and "Viva Cuba Libre". The crowd was there for her.

She barely heard Karl Decker's introduction which was appropriately formal and admiring and the crowd cheered again as, quite without knowing it, she took her place at the podium.

She remembered what it felt like to ride on the beach in Cienfuegos with Carlos when they were truly free.

She remembered what it was like to touch the soft leaves of a calabash tree. She remembered the way Cecilia had looked at her when she had come to tell her about her father, her irises yellow, the color of sadness.

Her voice was clear and strong as she began to speak. Her English almost perfect despite its accent. "I come to speak to you today," she said, "for the women and children of Cuba, who are helpless. The men, they speak for themselves, they defend themselves. But the women—the children—who are the victims of murder and outrage and who have lost husbands and sons, who have lost the men they love —must look to the great civilized government of the United States for protection.

"They ask—I ask this for them—that wholesale murder shall not any longer be permitted by Spanish troops and that you ask your Government to be their, our defender. As I stand before you today, I feel blessed that you have come to my aid, and I feel empowered by the ones that I have lost." She hesitated as if it were too difficult to go on. The crowd was silent, as if they were hanging on her every word. Katherine Decker had a moment where she felt disconnected from the crowd, was she the only one not caught under a spell, who still had the power of critical observation . . .

Onstage, Evangelina closed her eyes, as if she were trying to hold back tears, and then seemed to regain her poise. "To ask," she said, "that your Government come to the aid of all of us.

"As I stand on this soil, I feel protected by your beliefs, by your flag, and by the sanctuary you have offered me but I know that I will not truly be liberated until I can stand on the soil of my own country and know that every man, woman, and child is free. Viva Cuba Libre. Gracias." Drowning out her thanks, the crowd answered back to her, "Viva Cuba Libre."

Katherine Decker watched as the two of them stepped down from the stage into a waiting carriage. Karl lifting Evangelina in front of him, his arms around her waist. And then stepped into the carriage behind her. The door shut. The carriage took off. No hesitation, as if he didn't even notice that his wife was no longer at his side.

The crowd began to disperse, a sea of people, each going off to their individual lives. All that would be left was an empty stage and the brightly colored bits of confetti and long, thin ribbons of ticker tape littering the street.

$\mathcal{K}$atherine Decker arrived at Delmonico's a moment after the two "heroes," just in time to observe the crush of photographers waiting to record their entrance. As she stepped down from the carriage, Karl turned and saw her. He sent Evangelina on into the restaurant alone and waited for his wife on the sidewalk.

"We did it, Katherine," he said almost jubilantly.

"No, you did it, Karl. You and Miss Cisneros. I was not consulted."

And then their conversation was interrupted as Mrs. Logan, one of the gray-haired ladies who had taken up Evangelina's cause, descended on them. "You must be very proud," she said to Katherine as she took Karl Decker's hand.

"Yes, of course, I am," said Katherine wearing that professional smile again, "proud and relieved and quite exhausted, really."

They watched as Mrs. Logan walked into the restaurant leaving them momentarily alone on the street corner. "I have lost my place," said Katherine. "I no longer know how I am to behave. Am I to stand by your side, careful to insure that no one will detect that inside my heart is breaking?"

"Katherine, don't—

"Yes, Colin, it was thrilling," said Karl as Colin Metcalf slapped him on the back. "But not something I'd necessarily like to repeat. We'll be in, in a moment." He walked with Katherine down the street, so that they could have a little privacy.

"Are you going to tell me this is not a good time?" said Katherine. "I might make an appointment to see you. But how would I know that you would be there? There is never a good time for us." She stopped on the sidewalk and looked at him. "Am I to fight her? I will not. I will not be brought into a battle that I did not choose. My covenant with you," she said, as her hand found its way to her wedding band, twisting it, as if she were nervous, "was one that always excluded, what should I call it, 'complications,' my agreement with you, my commitment to you. My marriage to you was something I held sacred. Something that I thought no one could interfere with."

"Don't do this, now, Katherine. I can say nothing to you, Katherine."

She turned as if she was to leave him.

"I cannot ask you to forgive me," he said softly, so that no one could overhear them. "You cannot force an admission out of me. You cannot force me to say things that you do not want to hear. You cannot force me to speak about this . . . Katherine . . ." He called out louder than he meant to, "Katherine . . ."

But she had left him. Stepped into the waiting carriage and directed the driver to take her to Penn Station.

Contrary to anything Katherine Decker had said, she was a worthy adversary. And, she understood, almost as if she had been trained to it, that sometimes, the only way to fight for something was to walk away.

The banquettes were deep-blue velvet, tall white tapered candles were burning on all the tables and, as a centerpiece, white gardenias floating idly, fragrantly, in crystal bowls. The women were beautiful with diamond bracelets on their wrists and dresses that were the latest fashion, the men wore suits. The champagne, French and vintage, flowed freely. There were plates of lobster and shrimp and silver trays with fluted champagne glasses, all of which were full. There was laughter in the room and clever conversation. No expense had been spared by Mr. Hearst. The party at Delmonico's started shortly after the ticker-tape parade ended. Evangelina was exquisitely beautiful and well-spoken.

She no longer felt as if she were playing a part. She felt as if she had become what they wished of her, a symbol of her country's struggle, the flower of Cuba.

She looked across the room at Karl Decker, his profile strong and chiseled, a glass of champagne in his hand as he stood talking to two men and three admiring women. She did not see Katherine Decker anywhere in the room.

She remembered the first time she had seen him, when she thought his name was Charles Duval, as she sat at the pine table in the open prison yard at the *Casa de Recojidas*. How, at some point, she stopped "playing" him, stopped manipulating him, and started to trust him. It seemed so long ago, and, yet, it was only a month before. She had fallen in love with him. Did she have the right to fall in love with him?

She wondered what it would be like if she were to stay with him, remain in the U.S., accept the amnesty that had been offered to her. And, if she had the right to disrupt the course of his life, in that way, and hers.

She took another sip of champagne and then she felt someone take her arm. Julian Hawthorne looked down at her. "Are you overwhelmed?"

"A little. Thank you for asking."

"Would you like to step out on the street with me and get some air. There's something that I want to show you."

He led her to the front door of the restaurant and out onto the sidewalk. Across the street, above *The Journal*'s offices, an electric show of lights across a billboard, blinking on and off, THE JOURNAL WANTS A FREE CUBA!

She went to thank him and, in that moment, her English deserted her, as if the day had been too long, filled with too many emotions, and the words came out in Spanish, a torrent of effusive gratitude.

She got on her tiptoes and kissed Mr. Hawthorne on the cheek.

"When everyone in your country is free, Evangelina," he said, "then you will thank me." As behind them, the lights above *The Journal*'s offices continued to broadcast, at regular intervals, seeming to Evangelina almost as if it were a "sign," their message which could be seen twenty blocks uptown:

THE JOURNAL WANTS A FREE CUBA!

One lone carriage waited for them at the curb. The party had gone until almost two. They had lingered as the piano player played, for them alone, a Strauss waltz. They had not danced to it but rested, hunched over the back of the piano, as close to one another as they could, his hand lightly on her back, as they went over the events of the day, the parade, the speeches, the party. Neither of them mentioned Katherine.

The piano player began the simple strains of Debussy's "C'est l'Extase Langoureuse," composed for the Paul Verlaine poem, and began to sing softly the words, in French, as he played.

Karl took Evangelina's hand and led her to the dance floor. Her head rested on his shoulder, for a moment, as his other hand found its way to her waist. They stepped a careful distance from each other and began to dance. She felt light in his arms, his hand barely touching her back to lead her—although they were so much in step with one another that it was as if she needed no guidance from him, at all. For a moment, she caught a glimpse of herself dancing in his arms in the mirrored wall behind the dance floor, and realized, if she had her way, she would stay with him forever.

And, as the song began to end, the piano player sang softly, his voice low and perfectly accented, the last verse in French. If translated into English, the sense of the words would be:

The soul laments
This complaint which will always lay dormant.
It is ours, isn't it?
Yours, you say, and mine . . .
This humble story will always live
As it was told on this soft evening, almost
    silently.

When the music ended, it was difficult for him to let go of her hand.

A light snow was falling, even though it was early in the season, as if the air had suddenly turned as they went out onto the street. He lifted her again into the carriage. The streets were almost empty but the carriage driver navigated slowly, lazily, uptown, the gentle tapping of the horses' hooves across the cobblestones the only sound. Evangelina kept her face turned away from him, looking out the window. He took her hand.

She turned to look at him. Her voice was measured, as if she'd thought about what she was about to say. "Eduardo Cortez said to me, when I was leaving Havana, the choices you make now will be your own . . ."

He was very quiet. He waited for her to go on, but there was a way he looked at her that made it difficult for her to continue.

"Please, don't say to me," she said, "but I love you. For I would have to answer, 'And I love you, too.' "

She looked out the window again for a moment and then turned back to him. "Please don't ask me to stay with you, for I do not think I could refuse you anything.

"I have only one story, Karl. And you have many. But, I—" She hesitated as if she did not know how to phrase it. "There are so many of us who have worked so hard for this—that I must see what it becomes . . . Please don't say, 'I love you. . . .'

"To be with someone, really, I think you have to feel that you are always by their side, even if you are physically apart. That was how I felt—with Carlos. That is how Katherine feels with you. Please don't say, 'I love you . . .' "

She was crying now and he took her in his arms. Softly, she added, "Know that I will always love you, too." She pulled away from him and sat looking at him as if she were trying to memorize the way he looked so that she might never forget it.

And because it was for the last time and because they couldn't help it even if they'd wanted to, she let him take her in his arms and kiss her in a way that both of them would always remember.

It was snowing harder, now, flurries of white powder coming down around them. The carriage came to a stop in front of the Waldorf-Astoria, the awning of which was blanketed in white. The carriage driver opened the door, holding a large, black umbrella to shield her from the snow. Karl watched her as she got out of the carriage. He saw the slightest bit of ankle as she pulled her skirt up and stepped down into the street. She fairly ran across the walkway unmindful of the driver, the umbrella, or the snow. He remembered the way she'd run across the narrow boards, barefoot, high above the ground, to freedom, to the little house on O'Farrill Street, and the way she'd looked when he'd first met her, sitting at the rough pine table, alone, in the prison yard at the *Casa de Recojidas*, the way she'd whistled and everyone in the prison yard had frozen, the way she'd ridden before him in the mountains, so quickly that he could barely keep up, the way she'd stood before him on the ship, his arms about her waist, the spray from the ocean blowing across her face.

In the doorway of the hotel, she turned back to look at him, there were tears in her eyes, as she put a hand up to her mouth to say good-bye.

Viva Cuba Libre.

White Rose

Amy Ephron

A Reader's Guide

A Conversation with Amy Ephron

Q: How did you decide to write a novel about Evangelina Cisneros?

AE: When I first read about her, I felt as if I'd discovered someone. I was researching Princess Kaiulani (the last Princess of Hawaii). In an obscure biography of Kaiulani, there was a chapter that described the week that Kaiulani arrived in New York on her way to Washington to see President McKinley to make a plea, an unsuccessful plea, to save her country for her people. It was, curiously, the same week that Karl Decker brought Evangelina Cisneros to New York. The two women were continually mistaken for each other by the press and the public as they traveled through the city. There was a paragraph in the Kaiulani biography, where Kaiulani was quoted as having said, "The week that I was in New York, a true princess arrived in New York..." She went on to tell Miss Cisneros' story in four sentences. And I read it and realized that there was my next book. I am essentially a novelist and there were so many questions and contradictions in the accounts of Miss Cisneros' rescue, that a novel seemed the best way to write about her.

She seemed a true heroine—someone who, through no fault of their own, was thrust into a situation, the backdrop of the war, the fight for freedom for her country. She also struck me as being an oddly contemporary heroine since Hearst used her in numerous newspaper accounts to manipulate the feelings of women in America and sway public opinion to concur with his political sentiments that the Americans should help the Cubans obtain freedom from Spain. The subject intrigued me because it was about so many things—a beautiful young woman, imprisoned, whose spirit could not be broken, the power of the press, a newspaper reporter who was largely acting like a spy. And it seemed such an extraordinary story, that a young woman who had almost been lost in history, had been, in some way, the lynchpin that began the Spanish-American War.

Q: How much research did you do for the novel and how did you do your research?

AE: It's always important to me that I understand the period I'm writing about, the detail of the period: the clothes, the food, the politics of the times. You don't always research a thing directly, you sometimes go sideways of it. It was an enormous period of colonization, farming interests, pineapple, sugar, tobacco, and, even then, some notion of strategic military interest. It was during this period that the United States annexed Puerto Rico and Hawaii. It was also during this period that Marxist philosophy was becoming, for many countries and societies, a viable alternative.

I read a number of historical accounts of the Cuban revolutionary party at the time—about Maceo, Gomez, Betancourt, and the divisions within that party. I read Jose Marti's writings. I even went back to Samuel Morison's brilliant historical account in *The European Discovery of America: The Southern Voyages,* which detailed Columbus' second voyage when he mistakenly arrived in Cuba thinking it a limb of China, and spent months searching for gold and temples and returned home in disgrace. But it was then, in 1494, that he set up a column and a cross on the beach and officially claimed Cuba for Spain.

I also read a number of biographies of Hearst. Evangelina Cisneros appears briefly in many of them, as do accounts of "yellow journalism" and Hearst's attempts at the time to sway American opinion towards the possibility of a Spanish-American War.

I did some research using the Internet and occasionally hit Cuban web sites that detailed the revolutionary make-up of the party in Cuba at the time. And I unearthed a brief account that Evangelina Cisneros had written about her rescue, which gave me an insight into her voice, her spirit, and her sensibility.

The original newspaper accounts that ran in *The New York Journal* of her imprisonment and subsequent escape still exist, as does Pulitzer's debunking of those accounts. And I was fortunate to discover an extraordinary library, the Otto Richter Library at Miami University, which has a Cuban Studies desk.

I always knew that male-female relationships hadn't changed very much in the last 100 years. I was, however, startled to learn that Congress had twice turned down McKinley's request to send troops to Cuba (it wasn't until Evangelina Cisneros testified, that they finally agreed to allow him to send troops and the U.S.S. Maine), and that Congress' relationship to the President hasn't changed that much either in the last 100 years.

Q: Why do you think Evangelina was almost lost to history?

AE: I don't think Miss Cisneros' story was well reported, for obvious reasons, in Cuba—which was, at the time, officially under Spanish rule—although she was well known in revolutionary circles. And though she was a cause celebre in New York, the Spanish weren't happy about her, so her story was not well reported in Europe. We had no real global press then, there was no radio, no television, no CNN. And, I'm not sure why, but no one had ever written a book about her before.

In a way she was an obscure character. She was simply a political prisoner and there were many at the time, although her effect was extraordinary.

Q: **You showed restraint in the development of Evangelina Cisneros and Karl Decker's romance. It is primarily a story of an emotional affair and we are not given any overtly passionate scenes between them. It certainly adds to the elegance of the novel. However, do you think in the upcoming adaptation to film, this relationship will be sexualized?**

AE: I always think understated sexuality is more sensual in a novel. Their attraction, I think, permeates the book. I've had a couple of male reporters tell me that they fell in love with her. Obviously, on film, certain things will be more stated, but I still think understatement is more sensual than overt sexuality, even in a film.

Q: **Yellow journalism and William Randolph Hearst's critical role in it is obviously a focal point of this novel. Do you think any newspaper chain is capable of such influence today? Do you believe journalists of Karl Decker's ilk exist today? Why were journalists of this era so willing to "make" the news and risk their lives doing it?**

AE: What is classically termed "Yellow journalism" is really "making up" the news in order to sell newspapers. The slogan of *The Journal* was, "While others talk, *The Journal* acts." There is some evidence that Hearst "embellished" or allowed his reporters to "embellish," and in some cases makeup certain aspects of stories. His reporters also became involved in ways that would not necessarily be deemed ethical today. Not to propagate a conspiracy theory, but there was no CIA at the time, and I've always believed that many of the men who worked for Hearst were operating with the full knowledge of people in Washington and with instructions and permission to immerse themselves in their stories, as Karl Decker clearly did.

CNN certainly has enormous influence. We were all influenced by the images from Tiananmen Square. Journalists sway opinions in specific stories. Ruben Hurricane Carter comes to mind.

The Hearst I wrote about was younger than the one often portrayed and, I believe, operated from political conviction as well as a desire to sell papers.

Q: **The short vivid chapters of *White Rose* have a cinematic quality to them, almost like short takes, and a rapid cutting from place to place. Do you think this stems from your film background?**

AE: I don't write a novel thinking that it's a film. I think the best books are the ones you can get lost in, that you can picture as you read them. But essentially as a stylist, I'm a minimalist. And the roots of minimalism go back to Virginia Woolf, Isak Dinesen, etc. I like to play with language as it relates to place and time. And I spent a long time on Evangelina Cisneros' character, so that she would speak English, as she did, as a Spanish-speaking person speaking English, with sometimes odd inflections and oddly constructed descriptions.

Q: **You seem to have spent a lot of time on your secondary characters, particularly Katherine Decker. Many authors might have been content to relegate her to the stereotypical bin of turn-of-the-century New York society women. Yet, you gave her grit and a story, which brought another profoundly interesting dimension to the novel. Her own quiet brand of feminism acts as a subtle foil to Evangelina Cisneros. What does Katherine Decker represent to you?**

AE: I never think a triangle is very interesting (or ultimately satisfying or complicated enough) unless it's a fair fight between two women. Ultimately, a decision has to be made by someone, and if Evangelina Cisneros had not made it, I wonder, really, what Karl Decker's decision would have been. Katherine needed to be a formidable opponent.

American society women at the time were generally outspoken. Katherine Decker's quiet version of pacifism, her hesitance at embracing the notion of Manifest Destiny and Hearst's methods and motives, and her studied resistance to the notion of the U.S. entering a war that may or may not have been their business, echoes, I feel, modern sentiments that women often feel about war, and a political viewpoint that was certainly shared by some in 1897. In a way, she's the only one who had an overview, besides Eduardo Cortez. She was a voice that possibly closest echoes my own political sentiments and ambivalence about war, any war.

Q: Do you think there are similarities between the Elian Gonzalez' case and Evangelina Cisneros?

AE: In the way that they both captured the hearts of America and polarized opinions on both sides of the Atlantic, yes. In the way that they were both insignificant and yet wildly significant, yes. Do I think he ought to have been returned immediately? Yes. I was particularly struck by the children's march which occurred in Havana about eight weeks into his stay with his great-uncle, where all the children in Havana wore t-shirts emblazoned with a line that I believe is from a poem which said, "Who says a bird needs a gilded cage to sing?"

Q: You've spent time in Cuba. How were you affected by the country that you researched for so long?

AE: The Cuba that I wrote about is a Cuba that existed a hundred years ago—and yet a lot of it still remains. I spent a lot of time in Cuba retracing their steps, the steps of their escape. The Hotel Inglaterra, where Karl Decker stayed, still exists, almost unchanged from the way it appeared in 1897.

I think it's an extraordinary country, a tiny island on which there is a confluence of perfect architecture from the 14th, 15th, 16th, 17th, 18th, 19th, and 20th century. Spanish forts are still intact. The Riviera looks exactly the way it did the day Meyer Lansky walked out of it (except that the casino is now a dance floor). There are perfect Spanish palazzos, some of which have been converted to hotels, and perfect Art Deco buildings. There is a huge architectural restoration project presently ongoing in old Havana. And yet the city is largely unspoiled. It has held onto its character. There is also an extraordinary mixture of religions and culture. I love Cuba. I feel as if it's in my blood, somehow. In a way, it reminds me of Israel, particularly Jerusalem, this tiny island, curiously spiritual, that people have been fighting over for years.

Q: **Do you have any idea what your next novel will be?**

AE: I'm never sure what a book is until I'm deeply into it. But I think it will be a love story, an illicit love story, told partly in letters, that takes place over a 20-year period, set mostly in New York. And even though it has a vaguely historical backdrop, it's an original piece, not based on any real story.

Discussion Questions

1. Based on what you know about William Hearst and yellow journalism, do you think Karl Decker and Eugene Bryson embellished their accounts? Do you think Evangelina is not as innocent as they portrayed her and that there's a possibility that she led an uprising at the Isle of Pines?

2. What are your thoughts on newspapermen "making the news?" Are actions like Hearst's ever justified? It has been speculated that the newspaper moguls of this era were working in conjunction with the government. Do you believe that there is truth to this speculation?

3. Between the unique romance, a major historical event, and a good old-fashioned spy story, *White Rose* has something for nearly everyone. What elements of this novel drew you in the most?

4. This seems like a novel that can be enjoyed by men and women alike. Any thoughts on this?

5. Which characters intrigued you the most? Why?

6. This novel is essentially a love story, a triangle, hence the juxtaposition of the chapters with Katherine Decker in Washington, D.C. What significance did Katherine's perspective contribute to the story?

7. There are plans to adapt *White Rose* into a movie, and a rumor that Hearst will play a bigger role in the movie version. If you were the casting director, who would you choose to play the parts of Evangelina, Carlos, Karl, and Katherine?

8. Were you able to figure out the clues in the poem that

Evangelina wrote for Karl to help him break her out of prison?

9. Ms. Ephron's style is minimalistic. Did you feel the short, cinematic chapters transported you into late ninteenth century Cuba?

10. Do you think today's tabloid journalism is rooted in yellow journalism?

11. Have your read other novels or nonfiction about this period in Cuban history? If so, did you find consistencies in regard to the events depicted in *White Rose*?

12. What were your favorite moments in *White Rose*?

13. Can you think of other historical events and figures—that have not been previously mined—that would make for similarly exciting storytelling?

ABOUT THE AUTHOR

AMY EPHRON is a novelist, screenwriter, and producer. Her previous works include, *A Cup of Tea, Biodegradable Soap, Bruised Fruit,* and *Cool Shades.* Her most recent film was the 1995 adaptation of Frances Hodgson Burnett's classic riches-to-rags-to-riches children's book *A Little Princess.* Miss Ephron lives in Los Angeles with her three children.